THE LAST INVISIBLE BOY

written by
Evan Kuhlman

illustrated by
J. P. Coovert

ginee seo books
Atheneum Books for Young Readers
New York London Toronto Sydney

Atheneum Books for Young Readers
An imprint of Simon & Schuster Children's Publishing Division
1230 Avenue of the Americas, New York, New York 10020

Book design by Michael McCartney
The text for this book is set in Granjon LT.

Manufactured in the United States of America
First Edition   2 4 6 8 10 9 7 5 3 1

Library of Congress Cataloging-in-Publication Data
Kuhlman, Evan.
The last invisible boy/Evan Kuhlman ; illustrated by J. P. Coovert.—1st ed.
p.   cm.
"ginee seo books."
Summary: In the wake of his father's sudden death, twelve-year-old Finn feels he is becoming
invisible as his hair and skin become whiter by the day, and so he writes and illustrates a book
to try to understand what is happening and to hold on to himself and his father.
ISBN-13: 978-1-4169-5797-3   ISBN-10: 1-4169-5797-9
[1. Loss (Psychology)—Fiction. 2. Grief—Fiction. 3. Fathers and sons—Fiction.
4. Family life—Ohio—Fiction. 5. Schools—Fiction. 6. Ohio—Fiction.] I. Coovert, J. P., ill. II. Title.
PZ7.K9490113Las 2008   [Fic]—dc22   2007040258

To my parents and sister,
with love and gratitude

— E. K.

To my mom and dad,
for their endless love and support

— J. P. C.

1. A true story about a vanishing boy, part I

My name is Finn Garrett and this is my book and this is my story.

It is a story about losing something.

No, it's a story about sudden change.

Or it's the official autobiography of The Last Invisible Boy. Me.

There will also be some silliness, lots of my sucky drawings, a pop quiz and fun homework assignments, three or four family photos, and a few of my favorite memories. Caution: Sometimes the story will get a little sad. But it won't always be sad.

This book. It's like I'm driving a school bus but my legs are too short to reach the brake. It's a runaway bus so anything can happen.

2. A true story about a vanishing boy, part II

Once upon a time, in a magical kingdom, far, far away, I was a normal kid. I had shiny black hair that I wore kind of shaggy, and my skin came in one of the standard colors: fleshy pink. I was highly visible. I was just like everybody else. Went to school, played soccer, hung out with my friends and family. Dreamed of mostly stupid and impossible stuff, had few monster-sized worries. But that was in the past, before I began to disappear. Before that summer day when a giant eraser fell from the sky and flattened me.

The eraser quickly went to work. Attacked my hair, my skin, my smile. It's been erasing me from the world ever since.

Me before: Me after:

See the difference?

The truth? No giant eraser fell from the sky. That was just a dumb metaphor. Sorry. But things do fall from the sky and life can change that quickly. You'll be out walking one day, wondering why girls are so weird or what life in a black hole might be like, or maybe you're at home, bored and doing nothing, when BAM!—the meteor hits, the satellite crashes into your house and everything changes. The world has flipped upside down and then flopped over sideways, so good luck finding your way. You have no compass. You have no road map. You are on your own in a scary forest, so what do you do? Remember this: Even in upside-down and sideways worlds moss grows on the north side of trees. It will help you find your way out.

You may want to run, run, run to the past and hide there, but since you are from the present, the past will not have you. NO ADMITTANCE, KID says the sign on the door that you are trying to kick down, to find your way back to the day before the meteor struck. Keep kicking at that door. It probably won't work, but keep trying.

3. A true story about a vanishing boy, part III

I began disappearing this past June, right after what I call The Terrible Day That Changed Everything, the day I lost my dad forever.

That morning I looked in the bathroom mirror and saw that one strand of my black hair had turned milky white — its blackness had been erased — and that my skin was missing a small amount of pinkness, one of the proofs that I was a living kid. I had lost a little bit of myself. No, it was stolen. Nobody noticed but me.

Now people notice. Nearly half my hair has freakishly gone white and my skin is as pale as a ghost's. Call me Salt and Pepper Boy, or Frankenstein, or Snow White (if you are kind of mean), or Uncle Fester from *The Addams Family*, or Ghost Kid, or Count Freakula. I've heard it all.

I call what's happening to me "disappearing," even though I can still be seen. I'm that kid turning so brightly white you'll want to put on sunglasses. My thought: Dad was taken instantly. I'm vanishing in bits and pieces, like a disease that will not kill me but will erase me. First goes my hair and then my skin. And then the rest of me.

I am the bleached-out Nearly Invisible Boy. Going, going, gone.

4. My 10,000 lives

I turned twelve two weeks ago—don't be mad that you weren't invited to the birthday party, we didn't have one—but sometimes I feel like I've been living on this planet for hundreds of years. Been there, done that, a thousand times over. Do you ever get that feeling, that this is just your *current* life, that in previous lives you might have been a mad scientist, or an oak tree, or a curious frog, or a Viking explorer, or a painting hanging in a museum somewhere, or a freckled prince or princess? And that was just a few of your earthly lives. Remember those crazy days on Mars? Our summer vacation in a parallel universe? Or that year we bounced around in the asteroid belt, collecting rocks? Me neither!

But what if we all get ten lives or ten thousand lives, instead of just one? Ten thousand chances to be happy. How would you like to spend some of your thousands of lives? As animal, vegetable, or mineral?

If I were an animal I'd want to be a cheetah. Cheetahs are very fast.

If I were a vegetable I'd probably want to be broccoli. No one would want to eat me so I might get to live for a very long time.

If I were a mineral I'd want to be a big crystal, the kind that can turn sunbeams into rainbows. That is so cool.

5. Every name has a story

Finn is short for Findlay, which was also my great-grandfather's name on my mother's side. Great-Grandpa Findlay Harris was a lawyer who tried to keep innocent people from going to prison, and a congressman who fought for civil rights and equality for everyone. He made a difference. I want to make a difference.

So that's my first name, what's yours? Do you know the story behind it? For my names, Findlay is a Scottish and Irish name that means "fair hero" or "small blond soldier." I'm not a hero or a soldier, but my hair is turning a shade close to blond. A garret is a small room in the attic. Yep, that's me, a heroic blond soldier who lives in the attic.

I wasn't sure what Abner, my middle name, meant— I'm also named for Abner Harris, a great-uncle I never met—so I went online and looked it up. It's a Hebrew word that means "my father is light." Perfect. Absolutely freaking gigantically pie-in-the-sky, dance-until-next-July perfect. My father is light.

My family is currently made up of me and my mother Enid (her name means "soul") and my brother Derek (his name means "ruler of the people"—ha!) and my cat Henry (her name means "ruler of the house"—she thinks so!). That's right, Henry is a girl. I swear she looked like a boy when we found her at the Humane Society shelter. And she totally acts like a boy. She's lazy, just like me, complains about her food—I do this—sometimes pounces on people's heads for no known reason—something my little brother might do—and has all sorts of "attitude." Still, I have been seriously thinking of changing her name to Henrietta.

My mom is thirty-five, is very smart, and is a loan officer at Buckeye Bank & Trust. She is always busy, busy, busy. Here's a picture of her from two summers ago:

When my mother was a girl she liked ponies and lizards, and she collected stamps and baseball cards. She was very smart and once got a letter from the governor of Ohio congratulating her on her academic achievements. She still has that letter, but most of the stamps and baseball cards are gone. Here's a picture of my mom from her girl days:

Do you think she looks like me at all? Most people say I look more like my dad.

My brother is nine and is funny-looking. He hates to read, except for comic books, and he plays video games night and day. He often smells terrible, worse than the moldy basement, worse than me. Here's his second-grade school picture:

When he was three my brother fell off his tricycle and broke his arm. I laughed, seeing his arm weirdly bent, but Dad, being a dad, rushed Derek to the hospital. He wore a cast for like six weeks. Just about every kid in the neighborhood signed it.

My cat is about four years old and does very little besides sleeping and eating. Here's a picture from when she was more playful:

These days a dancing string just doesn't excite her.

That's all. Unless you want to know about my father, Albert Garrett. Every kid has to have a daddy, right, unless he was born in a laboratory or fell from the sky and landed on Earth and is pretending to be one of us.

Every kid has to have a daddy.

Every kid.

No exceptions.

So maybe I should tell you about my dad?

Noooooooooooooooooooo!

6. My father

Okay, you win, I'll tell you about my dad.

He was a good guy and a great father. He worked very hard at a job he didn't like much, managing a sporting goods store called World Champ Sports, at the mall in Ashton City. He was sometimes too quiet and sometimes too restless, wanting to be out in the world instead of at home with his family. But he loved his wife and his kids, and his dad and his brother and his sister, and he tried to take good care of them. And he loved baseball, too. Playing it and watching it and talking about it.

Now you know a little bit about Albert Garrett, my father. Albert, just so you know, means "bright nobility." Yep, that was my dad, all bright and noble.

7. Finn's pocket guide to time

I hate time. Don't you? When you want time to slow down, like when you are having too much fun, it speeds up. When you want it to go faster, like when you are bored or are having a bad day, it slows down. You just can't trust time. Not the past, not the present, not the future.

The past is every second of your life up until now. Up until NOW. See how quickly the present is gobbled up by the past?

The present is . . . Sorry, it's already gone. Hmm, it was just here a minute ago.

The future is every second of your life not yet written. It's tomorrow. It's twenty years from now. It is happening in one minute so sit up straight kid and look alive. But here's the stupid part. As soon as you arrive in the future it disappears and becomes the present, and then, before you know it, it's gobbled up and becomes your past.

And that is why I hate time. It's sneaky and tricky.

8. The log of the Starship Finn Garrett, entry I

EARTH DAY SEPTEMBER 16, 2:04 P.M. Home all alone, except for Henry the cat, but she's happily snoozing. Home all alone, like that kid in those old movies. Consider setting booby traps for klutzy burglars who will never show up. Not much crime in Sunnyvale. Shame.

Meanwhile, everyone else in the world is busy living their lives, at their job, at school, working the farm, jogging on a track, playing video games at an arcade. The planet keeps turning. The universe keeps expanding. But here I sit, doing nothing. Meet Nothing Boy, the non-superhero of Nothingville.

I really should be in school. It started three weeks ago but I haven't gone yet. Mom said to take as much time as I needed, so that's what I'm doing, taking my time. Weirdly, my brother Derek went back to school the first day. He seems to be doing pretty good, somehow, no loss of visibility, no evidence that he's being slowly erased. Or at least he's doing better than I am.

Why haven't I gone back to school yet? I think the main reason is because school was such a big part of Dad Is Still Here World that I'm just not sure I can make it work in Dad Is Gone World. Every year Dad would drive Derek and me to our first day of classes, and once or twice a week after that, tossing out fatherly advice like, "Study hard" and "Don't fall in love with too many girls." Now, it's Mom or the school bus. Then at night Dad would usually help my brother and me with our homework, though if it was math he would hand us over to Mom, saying, "Take that one to the banker."

Plus, kids at school are going to mess with me because of my weird hair and skin, I just know it. I hate being made fun of. Hate it, hate it, hate it.

5:12 P.M. Still have nothing to do. The day started sunny but the sun is gone. My little brother is outside, collecting bugs for his bug terrarium. Mom is fixing dinner. Fish sticks, fries, and something green and leafy and terrible-tasting and good for us. The cat is hiding somewhere.

I really need something to do.

6:40 P.M. I hate this time of day. Dad should be pulling into the driveway, home from work, late for dinner. Come inside, complain a little about his sporting goods store. Maybe some kids were tossing a football around and broke something, or a favorite employee suddenly quit and Dad had to cover his shift. Then maybe he'd tell us a joke he heard or just made up, something really stupid like, "Why did the dumb bee join the army? So he could shoot Stinger missiles." And then he'd give us some hugs and kisses. This used to be my favorite time of day.

8:01 P.M. Derek asks if I know where Mom is. We go hunting for her. She's not in any of the rooms or closets or storage areas or the garage. And she's not in the backyard, sitting on a lawn chair and watching the day go dark, like she likes to do. I look out front, see Mom sitting in the SMV (Soccer Mom Vehicle) but not doing anything. I give her a minute. I give her another minute. Then I go outside and knock on the car window. She rolls it down.

"Going somewhere?" I say.

"I must be," she says, looking kind of lost. "But where?"

Me: "To the store?"

Mom: "Yeah, probably to the store. I'm sure there are some things we need."

Me: "I think we're low on peanut butter."

My head: *You're the mom. You should know if we need stuff, not me.*

Mom: "It was definitely the store. But I guess I can go later, or tomorrow, right?"

She rolls up the window and slips out of the car. I take her hand and we walk to the house. Her hand feels bony and cool. It's weird when you remember that your parents are animals. Have bony hands. Are alive.

"That was strange," Mom says. "I couldn't remember going from the house to the car, or what I was planning to do."

"That happens to me all of the time," I say.

"Liar!" she says, smiling at me and looking more mom-like.

My brother comes flying outside and grabs Mom's free hand. Mom swings our arms back and forth like she's a happy mother with her happy kids. I wish it could last awhile.

9:34 P.M. Before Derek and I head upstairs we join Mom in the kitchen for a snack, strawberry toaster pastries from the health food store—Dad used to call them "mutant Pop-Tarts"—and soy milk. For some dumb reason Derek always cuts up his pastry with a knife and fork, but Mom and I eat them the normal way. So did Dad.

I must be looking a little down in the dumps because Mom runs a hand through my half-dead hair and says, "Cheer up. We made it through another day."

There's still two and a half hours left, I almost say, but I stop myself. Sometimes it's like I'm living my life, waiting for more bad news. When will I start expecting some good things to happen again?

"Can we get a monkey?" Derek asks. I almost laugh, imagining a monkey running through our house, knocking stuff over and swinging from the chandelier in the foyer. Thanks, Derek.

"Uh, let's think some more about that one," Mom says, which is her polite way of saying that we are not going to be getting a monkey anytime soon.

We finish our mutant pastries and soy milk.

9. A house on a hill in the center of the universe

My family and I live in a small town in the middle of Ohio called Sunnyvale. A vale is a valley but we don't live in a valley — this town is pretty flat, except for a few small hills. Our house is perched on one of those hills. That puts us a tiny bit closer to the sun and the moon and the stars and the rest of the universe than some of the other Sunnyvaleans. And a tiny bit closer to heaven.

During the summer the grassy hill is good for rolling or tumbling down, like old Jack and Jill, then running back up and doing it again. In winter the snowy hill is good for sledding or tumbling or backyard skiing (tape anything flat to your boots and see if they work as skis). And when it rains some of the neighbors who do not live on the hill growl at us for flooding their lawns. Sorry, not our fault. We did not design the Earth.

It used to always be sunny in Sunnyvale, even at night. But then one day I got mad at the sun for being so happy and for shining all of the time so I fired a BB gun at it and blew out some of its bulbs, and now Sunnyvale gets the same amount of sunshine as everywhere else. Believe me? A lie is when you twist the truth into a more interesting shape. Truth is made of clay. If it were made of stone you couldn't twist it, but you could break it.

If you broke it into many stones you could build a house out of it and live there by yourself, and everyone would leave you alone. *There was a boy who lived all alone in a stone house made of truth. He fell one day and chipped his tooth. "Ouch," the boy said.*

My house has three stories: stinky basement, sunny first floor, creaky second floor. I live on the second floor, suspended twenty feet above the Earth like a levitated kid at a magic show. This is what my house looks like:

This is what my room looks like. Sorry for the mess.

This is what my closet looks like:

The closet is the place I usually go when I want the world to disappear. A galaxy made up of me and some clothes and hangers to hold those clothes and board games and puzzles and shoes and boots and a 60-watt lightbulb, my mini sun. To activate the sun you tug on a string. Sometimes I stay in the closet for hours, thinking about my dad and other sad and happy stuff.

Or my little brother and I will slip into the closet and close the door and pretend we are in a spaceship hurtling through dark space.

"To Planet Kangaroo!" Derek might say.

"Loading the photon torpedoes and turning on the plasma shield, Commander," I might say.

Where we will land, who knows. A cold, dead moon? A living planet where kids are born smart so they can play baseball all day and never have to go to school? The 87th dimension?

If you are bored and need something to do, find a sketch pad or a notebook and draw a picture of where you live or write a poem about it. Do you like your house or trailer or apartment? Do you have your own bedroom or do you share your room with others? Do ghosts or night elves ever visit? If you could design your own house what would it look like? Do I ask too many stupid questions? Well, do I?

10. Beginnings

Before 1964 my house did not exist. Do you ever think about that, how everything in the world, including our planet, including you and me, including everything you own, had to be born or created?

Anyway, the land where our house now sits, the hill and the flat sections, used to be part of the neighbor's property. There might have been a small apple orchard on this land, or maybe this is where they kept the swimming pool or parked the old jalopy. But then my grandfather Victor (his name means what you think it would mean, "someone who wins"), who had just married my grandmother Nadine (her name means "hope"), bought the lot because he wanted to build a house in Sunnyvale.

My grandparents on my father's side, Victor and Nadine

Grandpa Victor didn't actually build the house, but he did help design it and he pounded in some of the nails, and he kept an eye on the construction workers to make sure they didn't goof off or do something daffy like forget to make any doors and windows. My grandfather designed the house to look like his childhood home in Crestline, Ohio, so unlike all of the other houses in this part of town it has a huge porch that surrounds most of the house and a porch swing you can waste half of the summer swinging on.

When the house was finished my grandparents moved in and raised three kids: Jacob, my skinny uncle (his name means "may God protect"), Meredith, my brainy aunt (her name means "great lord"), and Albert, who would eventually become my dad.

The house survived a fire in 1972 that was started when my dumb uncle Jacob lit a sparkler in the living room, then panicked and tossed it at the couch. Half the living room burned up. Today's important lesson: Do not light fireworks indoors. And the house survived a tornado in 1981 that tore off most of the roof, and many smaller storms. It's a strong house, but now it is also a sad house. It knows that someone is missing.

When the kids grew up and started their own lives, and after Grandma Nadine passed on, my grandfather sold the house to my dad, who had just met my mom at college and was ready to start his own family. My brother and I grew up here, spent most of our lives in this place. I like my house, and I think that most of the time my house likes me. It protects me from storms and cold weather. And it holds stories in its walls about every member of my family.

So the next time you go walking or skating or cartwheeling down the street, remember that each house or apartment building or trailer park you are passing has many stories to tell. Some of them happy, some of them sad.

Here's one of my house stories, written and drawn by me.

Day of the Terrible Storm, by Finn Garrett

During the summer my little brother Derek and I would spend part of every Saturday and Sunday watching the Cincinnati Reds games with our father. Just on TV, though Dad did once take us to a game, but I was little and don't remember much about it other than a foul ball whizzing over our heads, and that the drive to Cincinnati and back seemed to take forever. Dad worked crazy hours at his store but tried to make sure he was always home for the weekend games. It was so much fun. We'd wear our Reds caps and drink too much soda and eat too much junk food and root for the Reds and boo their opponents. The Reds needed our cheers — they pretty much stunk. Sometimes Mom would join us for a few innings but usually she'd do something else, saying she didn't want to "partake in such a primitive ritual." Mom often spoke funny like that.

One Saturday afternoon we gathered around the TV for a game, only to find out that it was postponed due to rain. Instead, Channel 7 was showing old Three Stooges episodes. I've always liked Moe the best. During one of the episodes the Channel 7 weather guy broke in to say that heavy thunderstorms "capable of producing tornadoes" were heading to Chauncey and Pickaway counties, which was a bad thing since Sunnyvale is in Chauncey County. He then showed the radar, and it looked like a big S-shaped band of mean storms was about to hit us, but when I gazed out the picture window all I saw was sunshine and nice weather. Said the TV weather guy, "Residents of Pickaway and Chauncey counties should seek shelter immediately. This isn't one to mess around with, folks."

I asked Dad if we should hurry down to the basement, but he said it looked like we had some time yet, and he gave my brother and me permission to go outside and search the sky for storm clouds. "But don't go far and come in as soon as it starts to rain," he said.

Derek and I ran outside and gazed at the sky. It was still a sleepy blue above us, but to the west ruffled purple clouds were racing the gray and white ones, and winning. It was a crazy sky painted by a nutty artist, too many different kinds of clouds and different colors all at once, some of the clouds and colors saying, *You are totally safe* and others saying, *You better run and hide!*

A blast of cool air then messed up my hair and the crisp smell of electric life filled my lungs. I loved how air smelled and felt right before and right after a storm, like nature was recharging its batteries. A billion D cells, or larger. There was a rumble in the west: Ashton City had been bombed, it sounded like.

"Woolah-hoo," I called to the storm. The storm's cannons answered with more thunder booms, one after another. "Woolah-hoo," I called again, and this time the storm responded with jigs of lightning, still pretty far away.

I kept my eyes to the west, to the coming storm. I remembered something my grandfather Victor had told Derek and me once, that to figure how far away a storm was you count the number of seconds it takes thunder to sound after the flash of lightning. "Remember boys, light travels faster than sound," he said. "A storm is about one mile away for every five seconds of difference." So I waited for the next lighting flash, then counted the seconds until thunder boomed. Only three seconds. The storm was getting close. It was time to go inside.

I looked for Derek but couldn't see him anywhere. He was the kind of kid who would wander away if you didn't keep a close eye on him. So I called my brother's name and then ran in the back.

Derek was there, in the backyard, trying to catch Henry the cat, but Henry did not want to be caught. She'd let Derek get close then dart away.

"Bad storm," my brother said.

"I know, but Henry will be okay," I said. "We have to go inside." Just then a bolt of lightning blew up a transformer attached to a telephone pole, a few streets to the south. Some of the noises of the neighborhood stopped and the one stupid streetlight that stayed on during the day went dead.

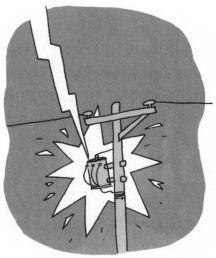

I took my brother's hand and pulled him toward the house. Sometimes he went along with it and sometimes he fought me, worried about Henry. As we reached the back door, rain started to fall in cool globs. I waited a few seconds before tugging Derek inside. It was a warm day and the rain felt good.

Inside the house, Mom was in the kitchen,

cleaning dishes, and Dad was in the living room, reading the weekly issue of *Sports Illustrated*. The power was out but there was still plenty of light to read by. "We better go downstairs," I said to my parents.

"Be right down," Mom said.

"You guys go ahead," said Dad. "I'll catch up." He kept reading his magazine. Even smiled and bobbed one of his legs a little like it was just a normal, sunny day. But in my head I saw a tornado swooping in and picking up my father and dropping him off somewhere in New Jersey. Dad still calmly reading his magazine.

Derek and I headed down the stairs, to the smelly basement. The first thing I did was twist on a flashlight that I found on a worktable, then I turned on the weather radio, to catch the latest updates. And Derek, as usual, buried himself in the clothesbasket, under a pile of dirty laundry. Extra protection against the storm.

Mom soon joined us. "When's Dad coming down?" I asked.

"I'm sure he'll be here any minute," she said, showing no worry. "I think he's still shutting windows."

On the radio the announcer said that a funnel cloud had been spotted somewhere near Highway 23, and that the storms had knocked down many trees. "Ten-four," Derek said, from deep inside the clothesbasket, even though the radio wasn't a two-way.

Winds shook the house and the sky went dark — it looked like night had moved in, seven hours early. Then hail attacked the roof and windows. It sounded like it was raining gum balls.

"I better get Dad," I said, starting for the stairs, but then Mom grabbed hold of my arm.

"No, no," she said. "I'm sure he'll be with us soon."

I pulled away from her, but didn't go after my father. The only proof that Dad was still alive and okay came a minute later when I heard him walking around upstairs, the beams of the basement ceiling creaking under his weight. Sounded like he was headed to the kitchen, maybe for a snack. Going for a cookie or some chips when he should be huddling in the basement with his family. It was one of those times when I hated Dad with all of me and loved him with all of me, at the same time. It was almost too much.

The storm smacked and punched and yelled at the house for another half hour. Dad never came downstairs. When the rain stopped and it started to become light outside and the weatherman on the radio gave the all clear, Mom and Derek and I headed upstairs. Dad was sitting in his easy chair, reading the same sports magazine.

"No biggie, just a little storm," he said, a weird smile screwing up his face.

Mom looked at Dad like she wanted to smack him, even though she's a nonviolent person, then she shook her head and went into the kitchen. Derek took a running start and then jumped onto Dad's lap and plastered him with what we used to call "slimy frog kisses." And I stomped upstairs to my room, furious that Dad had left us in the basement by ourselves during a dangerous storm, just so he could finish reading his dumb magazine. I found out later that two people in Circleville were killed in the storm when a big tree fell into their house. That could have happened to us, to my dad.

Dad never explained why he decided to stay upstairs during a fierce storm, but Mom said something kind of strange later that night, or maybe it was the next day. She said that sometimes men test themselves against things that are happening in the world, even natural things like storms. "A test of their manhood, or fortitude, maybe their willpower," she said. "It's one of their more primitive qualities, putting themselves in harm's way now and then just to see how they'll fare. It's ridiculous, very adolescent. Try not to be that way."

I didn't really understand what she was saying, but I nodded, pretending that I got it.

"So don't be mad at your father, okay?" Mom said. "He was just testing himself."

I told her I was no longer mad at Dad, even though I still was. He should have chosen a different test and joined his family in the cellar, safe from the storm.

I wrote that little story last spring, for a school assignment. Now, six months later, I have a different take on why Dad stayed in the living room while the storm rattled the house and his wife and kids hid in the basement. I don't think he was testing himself, he was testing us, see-ing how we'd do should the day come when he was no longer around to protect us. And maybe that's why what happened happened, Dad believing that we were ready to go on without him, even though we weren't. Perhaps we passed the survival-without-Dad test the day of the storm, but we are failing it now.

11. Finn's Amazing Water Tales, part I

If you shower six or seven times a day you will constantly dream about water. And soap. And rivers of shampoo. And rainstorms, in the house. And being naked and under attack by an army of water beads. And giant drains pulling you in and swallowing you up.

And your mom will say, "Don't waste all of the hot water!" And your brother will say, "I can't take a bath 'cause stupid Finn's still in the bathroom." And you will think of yourself as The Last Great Undersea Boy. Your arms have morphed into rubbery fins, and your hair is finely spun seaweed. Traded in your lungs for some nifty gills. Smart move, Undersea Boy. Or maybe you are an Olympic swimmer, faster than the rest. *And the winner of the gold medal for the 800-meter freestyle is . . .* Or a beached sea creature, dreaming of returning to his ocean home.

Mr. Goodman, my science teacher from last year, said that earthly life began in the sea, that we "clunky, air-breathing land-dwellers" owe our lives and our limbs to some brave fishes jumping out of the water a zillion years ago and giving life on shore a try. Grew lungs, eventually. Sprouted arms and legs over hundreds of thousands of years and crawled and then walked away from the sea and never looked back.

And Mr. Goodman said that the Earth is approximately 70 percent water, that, percentage-wise, sea life rules the planet. And he said that, quite amazingly, kids' bodies are also 70 percent water, though when they get older they drop down to about 60 percent, dry up a little. But even then we are still mostly water, each of us forever a Water Girl or a Water Boy.

Remember this, kid, and you will go far: The biology of the Earth is the biology of you.

And now a sensitive moment, sponsored by Kleenex. Need to cry your eyes out? Don't forget your Kleenex!

Sometimes when I cry — and I do way too much of that for a boy; I think there's something whacked with my crying machinery, like a stuck-open valve — I remind myself that I came from the ocean. Born in water and now I'm shedding some. But most times when I cry I'm too much of a blithering ninny to remember that important stuff.

No, I'm not crying right now, but thanks for asking. The last time I cried was two nights ago, watching a sad movie on Lifetime with Mom and Derek. A sad movie about a man who is killed by the Mafia in a case of mistaken identity, and the man's wife and his teenaged daughter, a girl with chipmunk teeth, have to learn to get by without him. Mom and I cried like crazy. Derek didn't cry. He almost never cries. He's a tough little kid.

The movie ended okay. The mom fell in love with a policeman investigating the murder, and she and her weird-looking daughter moved out of their little apartment in a noisy city and into the man's big house in the quiet suburbs.

"That would only happen in TV World," said Mom, blowing her nose and shaking her head as the movie credits rolled. "Where every ending is a happy ending."

I love happy endings. I just wish there were more of them.

12. Finn's Amazing Water Tales, part II

Mom says that I knew how to swim when I was a baby.
I can't remember back that far, my memories start when
I was about four, so I'll have to take her word for it. My
mother had signed me up for one of those infant swimming classes where they drop you into the water to see
whether you sink or you swim, and I guess I didn't sink
because I'm still here. "You swam like you had someplace
to urgently get to," Mom once told me. "A natural." I
sometimes wonder where I was trying to go.

At home I used to swim in a baby pool and in the bathtub. We have a video of Dad holding toddler me partway
into the bathwater while I thrashed my arms and kicked
my legs. Swimming, but not getting anywhere.

I love that video, watch it all of the time. I'm just starting out and have pink skin and charcoal black hair. Dad

looks so young and is bursting with energy and is happy, and Mom, behind the camera, is yipping encouragement. A whole, real, completely visible family. Except for my brother, soon to be under construction.

Now there's no room for me to swim in the bathtub, I just sit there like an overgrown goof. Like a fish out of water. We need a much bigger bathtub. Or a much smaller me.

But I can swim at the YMCA in Newbury Falls or in the roped-off area of Thompson Lake. I used to ride my bike to the lake all of the time, so I could splash around and build canals in the sand and chase gulls and sandpipers and stuff myself with ice cream and soft pretzels that I'd buy at the snack bar. It was always a blast. But these days I'm on a mission, hardly have fun at all. I like to swim until my arms feel like they are about to fall off, and my legs are wooden and heavy, half-dead. Swim until I'm so wiped out that all my body and brain want to do is sleep for a week. It's the only sure way I've found to clear my head.

Someday I will swim in the ocean. Make that every ocean and every sea. I will slip on scuba gear and discover a magical world of glow-in-the-dark fish and sea anemones. Find underground kingdoms, maybe, and the ruins of lost Atlantis. Recover trinkets and treasure from sunken ships and swim alongside spy submarines. I wonder if the eels and sea horses and octopuses and submarine crew members will think I'm weird.

Look out for the hammerhead shark, Undersea Boy! Yes, that's Undersea Boy, superhero for fishes and crustaceans.

13. The log of the Starship Finn Garrett, entry II

EARTH DAY SEPTEMBER 20, 1:35 P.M. I'm swinging on the front porch swing like a lazy kid bored out of his mind when Mom comes home, on a late lunch break from the bank. She parks the car then comes and sits with me on the swing.

"Hey there, Tex," she says, pretending we are cowpokes.

"Hey," I say, not playing along this time.

"You know," she says, "you'd have a lot more to do if you were in school. What do you say, ready to go back?"

"Maybe next week," I tell my mom. "I'll check my schedule."

Mom frowns at my smart answer then tells a story about when she was in college, two weeks from the end of the semester, and she got the news that her father, my grandpa Landon — his name means "long hill" — whom I never met because I didn't exist while he was still alive, had just passed away. I've heard this sad story before so I try to only half listen to it, but sometimes that's hard to do.

"After the funeral," says Mom, "I thought about dropping out of college, not just for the semester, but forever. My heart wasn't into it and I thought I could be of some help to my mother if I moved back home. But then I wondered what my dad would want me to do. Easy one. He'd want me to go back to school, get on with my life. Remember him, but still live my own life. So that was my plan. And it's a good thing I did go back to school because that's where I met your father."

Here comes the lesson part.

"So the lesson," Mom says, "is that sometimes you just have to soldier on. Return to your regular life and try to make the best of it."

"I know," I say. "Maybe next week."

Mom kisses me on the cheek then stands up, to head inside and fix lunch, I'm thinking. But first she gives me an invisibility check. "I don't think your hair has gotten any whiter," she says. "And your skin isn't too bad today."

It's true that my turning invisible has slowed down a little, but I'm sure it will pick up speed soon. "Must be all of those fruits and vegetables I've been eating," I say to my mom.

"That will be the day," she says, shaking her head and then going inside.

Just so you know, my mom's mother, Grandma Beatrice — her name means "traveler" — is still alive and is living in Florida. She must like it down there, seeing as how she has only visited us once in the past five years, and she only phones us during the Christmas holidays and on our birthdays. Some people just don't take their grand-parenting duties very seriously.

My grandparents on my mother's side, Landon and Beatrice

3:53 P.M. Look in the hallway mirror. *Hello, Freak Boy!* Try counting the white hairs, but there are too many of them. What is happening to me? Try remembering what my skin looked like when it was more fleshy, but that's not working too well. Try to remember what I was like before I started turning invisible. See a few flashes of that happy, normal kid I used to be. No genius, not a candidate for The Best Kid Ever, but he was okay.

Argh. I feel so weak and helpless here. An amoeba in a land of giants. Can't change the world. Can't bring my dad back. Can't even keep myself from turning invisible.

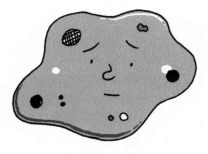

The new me

4:02 P.M. Consider raiding my saltwater taffy supply, really pigging out and giving myself a sugar buzz—that usually cheers me up—but my belly kind of hurts so I decide instead to work on this book. Would you like to meet Melanie?

14. So there's this girl . . .

Meli is a girl I know. She's twelve and her full name, Melanie, means "dark power." That is so wrong: She shines like the sun. Below is a picture of Meli in her Little League baseball uniform. She was the ace pitcher for the Royals this past summer. She also plays soccer and volleyball, and she's the star of the sixth-grade girls' basketball team at Sunnyvale Middle, the Mighty Hornets. I think they have won two games and lost one. I really should start going to her games, but these days I try to avoid places where lots of people have nothing better to do than to stare at my weird hair and skin. And if I ran into any of my teachers they'd ask me why I'm not in school yet.

What do you think? Be honest. Me, I dig her shiny green eyes.

Some people think that Meli is my girlfriend, probably because I tell them she's my girlfriend, but really we are just best friends. We plan to start dating in a year, when we are thirteen. Fourteen at the latest. Meli and I do sometimes hold hands, but most of the time when we are together we play board games and video games and sports, even football. I hardly ever escape her tackles, but she often slips away from mine. Melanie is better at most sports than I am. She's kind of a jock. And me? Dad used to say I was the "sensitive, artistic type." Great. I'd rather be good at sports.

And Meli is very sweet. She even picked flowers for me once, earlier this summer. Wild daisies and a velvety purple flower that I didn't know the name of. "Just because you're cool," she said when she handed me the bouquet. I kept the flowers in a Styrofoam cup full of water until they withered. The Styrofoam did not wither. It won't wither for hundreds or thousands of years. But flowers, due to no fault of their own, are not made of Styrofoam.

Can you keep a humongous secret? Melanie and I are planning to get married, either when we are eighteen, right after we graduate from high school, or we'll wait until we are done with college. We have lots of time to decide. Why does Melanie want to marry freaky little me? She says that I'm one of the few boys on Earth with more brains and sophistication than your average donkey. I'm not sure if that is a compliment, but I'll take it.

This is what Meli and I will look like ten years from now when we are married, and if I'm still visible:

And this is what we will look like when we are happy old-timers with a pile of stories to tell anyone who will listen:

I pray that happens, growing old with Meli. Holding hands and rocking in rocking chairs on a porch somewhere, sixty years from now and eighty years from now and one hundred years from now. Please, please, please, please, please, please, please.

And now you know why part of me, maybe even most of me, is fighting turning invisible — so I'll have a chance at a happy life with Melanie. I'm thinking most girls just don't go for invisible guys.

15. The world debut of Secret Agent Finn

Melanie is a fierce competitor when she's playing sports, but the rest of the time she's pretty cool. "Goodhearted" might be the word. Five days after The Terrible Day That Changed Everything she came over to my house and said, "Sorry about the you know." She wouldn't or couldn't meet my eyes, and she kept her hands in her pockets for the longest time, like she was afraid they would fly away if she let them out.

And I said, "Thanks, I'm sorry about it too," and then we played catch with a spongy football, or sometimes we punted it. Once when Meli kicked the ball it flew sideways off her foot and got caught in the upper branches of one of the maple trees. I pulled off one of my sneakers and threw it at the football to knock it down, thinking, *Gee, I hope my shoe doesn't get caught in the tree because I'd have to use my other shoe to try and free it.* It took ten or twelve tries before my sneaker smacked the football free, and fortunately the shoe didn't get tangled in the branches. "My hero," Melanie said, fluttering her eyelids.

We played for two more hours, tossing a football or a Frisbee or a baseball to each other, but not many more words were said that day. Meli and I both stink when it comes to talking about the big life-and-death stuff, at least with each other. I have no idea why that is. Wait, maybe I do know why. We don't want there to be any big life-and-death stuff in our lives, not yet. We want the world to leave us alone, let us be kids for a while longer. No big stuff allowed, please, only the small stuff. Too late.

When Meli had to go home for dinner I followed her like I was a spy, staying about a hundred feet behind her. Secret Agent Finn. All I needed was a trench coat and a Sherlock Holmes hat. I watched Melanie hop over a ditch and scratch her arm and brush her hair out of her face and kick at a bottle cap and say, "Hey there little guy" to a squirrel, and stop to tie her shoes and wave to one of her neighbors, Ms. Radcliff. I watched her cross three streets, once without looking both ways, gaze at the sky like she was checking it for flying saucers, and leap from a sidewalk square to another sidewalk square like she was trying to set a new world record in the long jump. That's one of her dreams, to be an Olympic champion or an otherwise world-famous athlete. And then she crossed into her yard and disappeared inside her house. I gazed at her house for a few seconds, hoping that her dad was going to be nice to her, that day and forever. He was always saying things to Meli like "You can do better," even when she was doing her best, scoring the most points in a basketball game or running faster than other girls. I hate her dad.

Where Melanie and her dad live

I learned something during my spying: Everyone has their own big and mysterious and beautiful life, and all of these lives are going on even when I'm not a part of them. Like with Meli—I'm lucky to spend one hour a day with her. That leaves twenty-three hours of every day where her big and mysterious and beautiful life goes on without me, and my big and mysterious and not-so-beautiful life goes on without her. Melanie and I really should be spending much more time together. Someday we will.

I am wondering now about your big and mysterious and beautiful life. You really should tell me about it. Take your time. I have all day.

16. Let's all act like we're normal

I went to school today. I wasn't planning to go for another week or two, maybe three, but I really didn't have any choice.

Yesterday a man from the school district came to our house and told Mom that I had to start attending classes or I'd have to repeat sixth grade. "I'd truly hate to see Findlay held back," said the man, scratching his big honker of a nose and looking like he couldn't care less if I had to repeat the year. I don't want to repeat this year, but maybe the one before that or the one before that or the one before that or the one before that or the one before that or the one before that or the one before that or the one before that or the one before that or the one before that.

Our visitor wore a short-sleeve shirt and I could see his bony elbows. They weren't happy elbows. His brown trousers were nerdishly two inches too short—flood pants— he was missing most of his reddish brown hair, and he had three jagged worry lines scribbled across his forehead. I wondered what his big and mysterious and beautiful life was like, if he was having any fun, and what his life was like when he was my age. I guessed that he was a misfit, like me, a freak, but who knows, he could have been one of the normals.

Mom said, "You understand, don't you, that it's been difficult for Finn? He and his father . . ."

Man said, "Yes, of course. I'm not without sympathy, we've all had rough patches we've had to endure, but policy is policy."

And I said, in my head, *Policy is policy is policy is policy is policy.*

And now I'm back in school.

I wasn't in the mood to ride the smelly bus, a hundred burrowing eyes aimed at me, so Mom drove me to school in the SMV. When she pulled in front of Sunnyvale Middle and stopped the car I told her that I thought I was going to be sick, that we better turn around and head home.

"Are you sure?" asked Mom, trying very hard to look strong and parentlike, but I wasn't really buying it. "You're going to have to face the music eventually."

"I'm pretty sick here," I said, wondering if I should throw in a long groan.

"Okay, no problem," Mom said, looking a little bit sad. "Let's try again tomorrow."

But as she started to pull the SMV away from the school I saw a herd of kids heading inside the building for the start of classes. I wanted to be part of that herd.

"Wait," I said. "I'll give it a try."

"Tomorrow might be better," Mom said. "After one more day of rest."

"No, I want to do this," I said. "Today."

Mom stopped the car and then gazed at me. Her eyes were a little wet. "In that case, here's some advice," she said, "something I learned when I went back to college after your grandfather passed away. Just smile and keep smiling and that yucky feeling will go away."

"That works?" I asked.

"Give it a try," Mom said.

So I slid out of the car and made my way to the front doors of the school, blending in as best I could with a different herd of kids moving in the same direction. I smiled and kept smiling and that yucky feeling started to go away.

When I was a few feet inside of the building Meli launched herself at me and gave me a huge hug, which turned out to be a very awkward hug since we were both wearing our backpacks. "My sweet prince returns!" she said, kind of loud.

I think I might have blushed a little, even with my pale skin. "I'm happy to be here," I said, which was only half a lie.

Everyone else was pretty nice to me, saying things like "How are you?" and "Nice to see you, Finn," and "Sorry about what happened" and "Nothing personal, but you look pretty weird." My friend Benjamin, his name means "son of the right hand," was one of the kids who asked why I looked so pale and what was up with my hair. I didn't really know the reason for my growing invisibility so I didn't answer, but then later I thought of an answer. My box of crayons has been stolen from me. Every color, gone.

Except for black. Except for white.

17. Finn the living ghost

In gym class, while watching kids play softball—I didn't bring a pair of gym shorts so I wasn't allowed to participate—I thought of another possible explanation for my invisibility: I'm slowly turning myself into a living ghost so I can hang out with my dad. It takes a ghost to find a ghost, right?

This thought goes back to The Terrible Day That Changed Everything, when my mother and brother and Grandpa Victor and I were returning home from the airport. We were stopped at a red light, a few miles north of Sunnyvale, when Vic looked at me and said, "Your father is with us now and will always be with us. Don't ever forget that. You too, Derek."

"He's like a ghost?" my brother asked.

"Sure, why not," Grandpa Victor said. "Ghosts can go anywhere they want, and Albert chooses to be with his family. He's with us in this car, I'd swear to it."

Mom sighed but didn't say anything. She has never believed in ghosts or UFOs or Bigfoot or anything that scientists can't prove the existence of. And I looked around for my dad but couldn't see him, nor did it feel like he was riding with us in the car. Whenever Dad was in the car, at least when he was driving, there was always a sense of possibility, like we could unexpectedly end up at a toy store or a pizza shop or a go-cart track. *But maybe that's how* real *ghosts are,* I thought, *not at all like the ones you see in movies and on TV.* You can't see them or sense them but they are still there, keeping watch over the people they loved.

Anyway, that's what I was thinking while watching the kids play softball — kind of ghostlike, I was watching them but they weren't watching me, that I was turning myself into a living ghost so I could hang out with my dad. It sounded like the perfect life. Be with Dad. Play catch all day. Follow people around like we were spies. Go to every Reds and Bengals game, since ghosts get in for free. And talk about stuff, including the things I wish I could have told Dad before he left us. Like that I loved him. Like that he was a great dad. Like that I will miss him every day of my life. Just me and my dad, alone in our own mini universe. And since we'd be invisible no one could ever mess with us. Not once, not ever. The perfect world.

But now that I've had some time to think about it I'm just not sure that I'm turning myself into a living ghost, especially since I'd only want to be a part-time ghost. Visit my Dad, play jokes on some people, then become visible again so I could spend time with Meli, and Mom, and Derek, and Henry the cat. So maybe there's a better explanation for my invisibility that I just haven't thought of yet.

Any ideas, even really weird ones?

Do you like this book so far? My next book will be called *The Process of Invisibility: Can It Be Reversed? Should It Be?* I think it will be a runaway bestseller, since just about every kid has felt invisible at some point. Have you? Maybe in a crowded classroom? Maybe at a busy store? Maybe at home when no one is paying attention to you? Fight invisibility! Jump up and down if you have to. Shout, *I'm here, I'm here!*

I'm pretty sure I'm the first kid to physically turn invisible. Lucky me. But at least the battle between Visible Boy and Invisible Boy is a close fight. I have lots of white hair but also lots of black hair, and my skin isn't totally zombie white, not yet. It's like a baseball game tied 3-3, going into the seventh inning. Who knows which team will win? Like Dad used to say when the Reds were getting clobbered by the Cardinals or Braves or Mets or even by the Marlins, "It ain't over until it's over, Rover." Sometimes even lousy teams rally at the last minute.

And as of this ticking-away minute ... I'm here, I'm here!

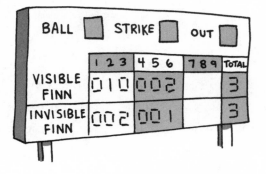

18. Invisible you

If you were granted the power of total invisibility for a day how would you use that power? Maybe spy on your crazy neighbors or your friends? Sneak into movie theaters? Visit the White House and try to spook the president's dog? Hide all of your sister's clothes?

Make a list of six or eight fun things you'd do while invisible. I hope, Temporary Invisible Kid, that you will use your new powers only for good. Or mostly for good?

19. Back at School

In earth science class we played with microscopes.

Here's a look at human hair (Benjamin's), a bitten-off chunk of finger-nail (mine), a leaf from an oak tree in the schoolyard, shed gerbil fur (from Sammy, the science class gerbil), and a human tear (could be mine):

In art class Ms. Lee handed out charcoal pencils and construction paper and said we could draw whatever we wanted to draw.

This is what I'll look like when I'm forty-eight, assuming that my visibility has been restored:

This is what I'll look like when I'm reincarnated:

This is what I looked like when I was still a normal kid:

In the hallway Jerry, the always-cheerful assistant principal at Sunnyvale Middle, a man with a big smile painted on his face, but not in a clown kind of way, said, "Welcome back to the zoo," and then he asked how things were going.

"Fine," I said, not feeling even close to fine. "How are you?"

"Fine also," he said, "except for a tiny toothache."

I told him that my mom rubs clove oil on my gums whenever I have a toothache and it takes the pain away.

Jerry said, "Thanks for the hot tip."

"You're welcome," I said, thinking that Jerry and I were having one of those dumb conversations where we were talking about unimportant stuff instead of The Big Horrible Thing That Happened Back in June.

Before heading to my next class I asked Jerry if he knew what his first name meant.

"I believe that Gerald means 'rule of the spear,'" he said, some shyness in his eyes. Another name that didn't fit.

"That's exactly you," I said, walking away.

20. Intermission

Here's a comic strip I drew during boring world history class. I fixed it up when I got home. Hope you like it.

Does Anyone Speak My Language?

21. Mystery meat

At lunch I sat with Benjamin and a few other guys, mostly seventh graders, at one of the tables set aside for outsiders and middle-of-the-road kids, the ones neither popular nor much made fun of. Invisible, but only in the social way. I used to be a middle-of-the-road kid, but now with my freaky looks I'm definitely an outsider. Hooray.

While I was busy sawing through a hunk of mystery meat, today's nutrition-free lunch, a kid named Russell Lansky handed me a pack of vitamins that his mom had slipped into his lunch sack. "I think you need these more than I do," he said. I thanked Russell and tried the vitamins, but they didn't seem to fix me. Russell, in French, means "little red one."

And then a seventh grader named Rachel Castleman, kind of dark and Gothy but not overly fond of vampires, came up to our table and asked me which beauty salon I went to for my "extreme" dye job. "It looks totally retro zombie," she said. "I love it." Rachel, in Hebrew, means "ewe," a female sheep.

I told her I did my hair myself, thanks for asking.

After Rachel stole one of Russell's carrot sticks and then left with a shrug, Benjamin said that I should have asked her out. "I think she likes you," he said. "She was totally looking at you that way."

"She just likes my freaky hair," I said.

"It is pretty weird," he said, glancing at my black and

white cowlicks. "I've never seen hair that color before, except on adults."

"I'm an experimental kid," I said. "The first of my kind."

Ben, unimpressed, went back to eating. I thought about telling him about my turning invisible but I didn't want to upset him. Ben doesn't have many friends. He'd be sad to see me go.

In math class Ms. Morton, one of our many semi-burned-out teachers, was worried about my pale looks so she sent me to the infirmary to see Nurse Glenda.

"Oh dear Lord," said Nurse Glenda, looking at me like a two-headed kid just wandered into her little room. "Are you feeling okay? Do you need to lie down?"

"You tell me," I said. Sometimes I can be a real smart-mouth.

Nurse Glenda had me stick out my tongue and say "ahh," and then she took my temperature: 97.9. She said I was running a little cool. I heard it as *Run, you little fool,* so I jumped up and ran out of the infirmary. Glenda, I found out later, means "pure and good."

I got lost on the way back to math class. I wasn't even sure I was in the right school. I wasn't even sure I was on the right planet. It was like one of those dreams when you are at your school, and most kids and teachers and things look pretty normal, but something isn't quite right. Maybe you are only wearing your Spider-Man underwear from a long time ago and Abe Lincoln's stovepipe hat, or the locker combination numbers are in hieroglyphics, and you just know you are going to be very late to class.

And then room 312 magically appeared. I opened the

door and slipped inside. There were so many visible kids, their skin as pink as bubble gum, as brown as chocolate, as yellow as corn silk. It was beautiful. I almost cried. I used to be one of them.

A few kids stared at me for nearly the entire rest of the class, in the "Who is that freak?" kind of way, not in the better "Who is that handsome kid?" kind of way: Carley Barnes and Myles Teasley and that new girl, the one with the ringlets and the braces. I think her name is Rhiannon. Catching a glimpse of vanishing Finn Garrett while they still can, before he goes totally stealth and unseeable. At my current rate of erasure it could happen any day now. But I'm not ready to be invisible! I need a rain delay. I need a cure.

In case you're keeping score at home, Carley is a German name that means "army" or "warrior," Myles is a Latin name that means "soldier," and Rhiannon is a Celtic name that means "great queen."

If you're not keeping score at home, what gives?

22. A look at the weather

Today's weather summary, starring Nearly Invisible Finn, the half-kid, half-hologram Channel 7 weather guy: The sun shone all morning, and then it stormed, and then the sun came back out. The sun wins!

Tomorrow? Expect more weather.

The end. Go to commercial.

Hi, kids. Tired of feeling like an elephant that swallowed a cow that swallowed a pig? Try Diet Wheat Bran Yummies today. Composed of nearly 100 percent sugar, Diet Wheat Bran Yummies will help you burn off every fat cell in your body. You'll become absolutely skeletal! Practically see-through! Yes, that's Diet Wheat Bran Yummies. An important part of an imbalanced breakfast.

End of silly moment.

23. Headshrinking with Dr. A

After school I met with Dr. Amanda, the school district psychologist. Amanda in Latin means "lovable." Every one of us should be named Amanda, even the guys. I'm going to be seeing Dr. Amanda once a week. It's one of those "I know you're not going to like it but shut up and do it anyway" things.

As soon as I sat down on a cushy little chair Dr. A asked about my weird hair and snowy skin. I didn't tell her I was turning invisible—it's not something most adults would understand—but I did admit that almost every day my hair and skin get a little bit whiter. "It started as one white hair, right after it happened," I said. "I think there are now more white hairs than black hairs. I think I might be losing."

And Dr. Amanda said, "Sometimes when we experience a severe emotional shock we react in unexpected, even unique ways. The workings of the mind, despite all of the scientific advances we've made, remain a huge mystery."

And I said, "So this is all in my head?"

And she said, "Or perhaps in your soul."

And my head said, *So that's why I'm turning invisible. My soul has been smacked.*

And then Dr. A asked me what I thought death was like.

And I said next question please.

And she said let's try answering this one first.

And I said that death is when you are no more, like a notebook that runs out of pages. Toward the end, I told her, I will write very small and in all of the margins. Keep it going. And when I get to the last page I will ask for a new book to write in. Something with Pegasus on the cover.

"Why Pegasus?" Dr. A asked.

I thought about my answer. "Pegasus had really big wings," I said. "He could fly anywhere he wanted to."

"Feel like you want to escape from your troubles?" she asked. "Fly far away?"

"Sometimes," I admitted.

Dr. Amanda then offered me some graham crackers and a juice box: Granny Smith apple. I wolfed down four crackers and slurped some juice. They were just what I needed to calm my gurgling stomach.

And then our first session was over. I survived it. As I was leaving Dr. Amanda winked at me in the "you're okay in my book" kind of way. I normally only get that kind of wink from Mom, and sometimes from Melanie, but other times Meli's wink is the different kind of wink, the kind that can make me accidentally walk into a tree. Winks can be ultra confusing.

24. Pegasus factoids

1) Pegasus is the winged horse from ancient Greek mythology. Nearly every god and mortal wanted to catch him and ride him, but, having wings, he was pretty good at escaping.

2) Pegasus's dad was Poseidon, the god of the sea, and his mom was Medusa, an evil Gorgon who had fangs and lizard skin and living snakes for hair. And you thought your family was weird.

3) Pegasus was born out of Medusa after the hero Perseus, who was wearing an invisibility helmet that Hades, the god of the underworld, had lent to him, snuck past other Gorgons and sliced off Medusa's head with a sword while she slept. Since he was still invisible Perseus easily escaped. On the way home he saved a lady named Andromeda from a sea monster and then married her.

4) Pegasus's job was to carry lightning bolts for Zeus, the king of the gods.

5) One day when Pegasus was hanging out on Mount Helicon he kicked at some dirt and uncovered a spring that became the source of inspiration for all poets and writers. Good thing he did that or this book might not exist.

6) According to the myth, when Pegasus died he became a star constellation. Perseus also has his own constellation.

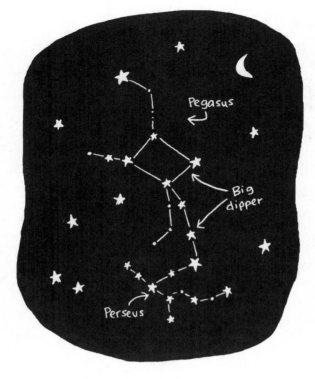

7) Pegasus is not the only mythological hybrid animal. Others include griffins (half lion and half eagle), centaurs (half human and half horse), and Minotaurs (half man and half bull).

25. The log of the Starship Finn Garrett, entry III

EARTH DAY SEPTEMBER 26, 4:45 P.M. Back home. In my room. Unloading my stuffed backpack. I have so much homework to catch up on it's not even funny.

Complete backpack contents: math book and workbook, history book and study guide, a stack of school papers to sort through, a notebook and a sketch pad, a novel called *The Red Badge of Courage*, five pens and one regular pencil and one charcoal art pencil, a mini calculator, a cheap MP3 player that usually doesn't work, a cell phone for emergency use only (thirty-five cents a minute!), a pack of Juicy Fruit gum (one stick missing), three dollars and eight cents, a piece of paper with phone numbers and a few e-mail addresses on it, a picture of Melanie crossing her eyes and trying to look like a weirdo, two emergency pieces of salt-water taffy, and a Ken Griffey Jr. baseball card in a plastic sleeve. He's my favorite player, though Dad once said that Ken's dad, Ken Griffey Sr., who used to play outfield for the Reds, was a more reliable ballplayer, because he was hardly ever injured. Dad's favorite Reds player of all time was a catcher named Johnny Bench. He could really smack the ball, my dad said.

Crap. I need to get some work done. Later.

26. There goes dinner

We were supposed to have chicken potpies for dinner, but while I was doing my homework and Derek was outside playing and Mom was doing whatever she was doing, she totally smoked the pies. I thought I smelled something burning downstairs, but usually when there's trouble in the kitchen the smoke alarm goes off.

"I was sure I set the timer," said Mom, looking worn out and spacey as she scraped the foil tins and charcoal crusts and dark goo into a wastebasket. "I must be losing it."

You and me both, I thought.

So Mom made tuna fish and cucumber sandwiches instead. Derek and I didn't really care, we like tuna fish and cucumber sandwiches. But Mom, all of the way through dinner, just didn't look like herself, like only a thin string was stopping her from falling apart.

Keep it together was my other big thought, for both Mom and me.

As we were finishing supper my grandpa Victor, Dad's dad, stopped over for a surprise visit. He was carrying a toolbox and said he wanted to make sure the house was in "shipshape" condition. He went from room to room, tightening bolts and screws, checking plumbing fixtures, making sure the furnace filters didn't need to be replaced, that kind of stuff. Derek and I followed Grandpa Vic around for a little while, but then Derek got bored and I had to get back to my homework. I do know that later on Vic went outside and checked the air pressure on the tires of the SMV, and then he poked around under the hood. He told Mom that the car needed a new air filter and that he'd pick one up at the auto parts store tomorrow.

"That was nice of your grandfather, to help us out like that," Mom said after Vic was gone. But something in Mom's face was telling me that she, like me, was wondering if Grandpa Vic was really worried that our house and car were falling apart, or if he was just bored and sad and needed something to do.

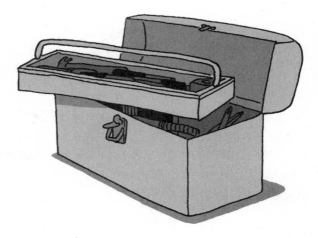

27. The log of the Starship Finn Garrett, entry IV

EARTH DAY SEPTEMBER 26, 10:14 P.M. Still doing my homework. The door opens. It's Derek, holding his sleeping bag and pillow and his stuffed hippopotamus. My brother looks at me to see if I'm going to yell at him to get the hell out, and when I don't he comes into my room, closes the door, sets the sleeping bag and pillow on the rug, then plops down and slides inside the bag, clutching the toy hippo. He used to go to sleep on Mom and Dad's floor when he was feeling a little lonely or if he was worried about nightmares. Now he comes to me.

"Good night sleep tight," Derek says.

"Good night sleep tight," I say.

"Of course," he says.

Just as my brother is closing his eyes I toss a piece of saltwater taffy his way and end up bonking him on the head. Oops.

"Ouch," he says, rubbing his skull, then he picks up the piece of candy and examines it. Peach-flavored taffy, not exactly my favorite. "This is your gift, not mine," he says.

"I'm sharing it," I say.

"Oh." Derek sits up and unwraps the candy and slips it into his mouth. He chews the taffy in a loud and sloppy, horsey kind of way. It looks like a big chore.

When my brother is done with the taffy he says thanks

then sets his head back on his pillow. "Are you going to be throwing anything else at me?" he asks.

"Probably not tonight," I say. "Good night sleep tight."

"We already did that," he says.

What I know: In ten minutes Derek will be up on my bed, sleeping while I'm doing schoolwork, or I'll be on the floor, telling him a make-believe story involving harmless monsters or talking animals. Or we'll head into the space capsule and travel to a place in the universe we haven't been to before. In or out of the space capsule sometimes there is only us.

I better go now. Bye.

28. Midnight baseball

When my father was a kid he dreamed of becoming a pro baseball player, or at least a coach. He chased that dream through Little League, Pony League, high school, and into college before giving it up after meeting the woman who would become my mom. Dad decided that he wanted to be a family man, that being on the road six months out of every year, as a player or a coach, was not the life for him.

But he held on to his love of baseball. He'd follow the Reds every year, and he'd often play catch or hit the ball with Derek and me, even though my brother and I weren't exactly star athletes. One time we even played catch with Dad at two in the morning. That night — it was a steamy night in early July, the summer before this past one — Dad surprised Derek and me by waking us up and announcing that we were going to go play ball at the city diamond where the Little League games were played.

"I'm sorry that I've been such a lousy dad lately," Dad said while in my room, waking me up. "Let me try to make it up to you and your brother." As far as I knew my dad had been a pretty good dad lately. Worked too hard and played too little, sometimes complained about stupid stuff, but wasn't that true of most adults?

I sat up and looked around. "It's dark out," I said. "We won't be able to see the ball."

"Sure we will," Dad said. "They leave the lights on at the park all night. Come on, it will be a gas."

I slipped out of bed, and as I was putting on jeans and my Cincinnati Reds T-shirt, my father left to wake up Derek. When my brother was dressed we gathered our mitts and two baseballs and three bats and loaded that stuff and ourselves into Dad's Chrysler.

"Does Mom know about this?" I asked as we were backing down the driveway.

"This one is a men-only adventure," Dad said. "So let's keep this one under our hats for now. Okay?" Derek and I both nodded.

It was only a five-minute drive to the ball diamond but that was plenty of time for my brother to fall asleep, his head resting on my bony shoulder. I, on the other hand, was wide awake. Being someplace other than in my bed at two in the morning was something new and exciting.

When we were about halfway to the park Dad said, "This is the kind of father I want to be—midnight baseball!—not that other kind: absent, self-absorbed. Cranky."

"You're doing okay," I said.

"Sometimes yes, sometimes no," he said. "But I can do better."

When we arrived at the diamond we saw that all of the field lights were turned off, that only a small amount of light was coming from a streetlamp that hung above the parking lot, and it looked half asleep.

"I swore they kept the lights on all night," Dad said, looking like he was doing some serious thinking. "Oh well. If life throws you a curveball you better know how to hit curveballs."

"How do you hit curveballs?" I asked, really wanting to know.

"You swing where the ball is going to end up, not where it appears to be headed," he said. "You have to trust your instincts instead of your eyes."

Then my dad pulled the car up to the fence that keeps people and dogs from wandering onto the field during games, sort of angling the car so the headlights lit up most of the infield. "That should do us fine," he said.

I woke up Derek and we all climbed out of the car, clutching mitts and bats and baseballs, the headlights on the car still burning bright so we could see what we were doing. We took the field, first tossing a ball back and forth to each other to warm up. Derek looked a little droopy but I was having the time of my life, playing catch with my dad and my brother while just about every other kid in Sunnyvale, in all of America, was sleeping.

Next, Dad hit grounders to Derek and me, and sometimes pop-ups. Occasionally the ball skipped or flew past us and ended up in the dark zone, the outfield. One time it took a good three minutes to find the ball. Half of the moon and lots of stars were shining above us but they didn't provide much helpful light.

While my father was still at home plate, hitting the ball to Derek and me, Mom pulled the SMV into the parking lot and headed right for us.

"Busted," Dad said, losing his smile.

Mom jumped out of her car and ran to Dad and yelled and pointed a finger and might have even stomped her feet. "Are you insane?" she said. "I thought you all had been kidnapped, or worse! If I didn't find you in the next minute I was headed to the police station."

"Sorry," said Dad, looking like he wished he were a turtle instead of a person and could retreat inside his shell. "This was just something I really needed to do. I haven't been much of a dad to the boys lately."

"Then tell me about your plans or at least leave a note,"

Mom said. "I was worried half to death!" My parents almost never yelled at each other, but when they did fight Mom usually did most of the screaming, which I think made her even madder, that my dad would never put up a decent fight.

Dad apologized again then told Derek and me to "pack it in" as he went to start his car. But keeping the headlights burning all of this time had drained most of the juice from the battery. So Mom, even though she wasn't too happy about it, had to give his car a jump.

When the Chrysler was running Mom said, "Come on, boys," like she wanted Derek and me to ride home with her, but my brother and I rode with Dad. Nothing against our mother, but this was a men-only adventure. Mom was pretty steamed with Derek and me, but that wore off by the next morning.

My dad had some things to say on the way home, but I was too sleepy to record them all. But I do remember that he said this: "Sometimes you just have to freewheel it, take a right turn instead of the standard left turn and see what happens. Turkeys might be happy living the same day again and again, but people aren't turkeys. We need that occasional right turn just to see what's out there." When we got home I wrote those words in a notebook that would become my first journal. They sounded really smart, something I'd want to think about when I was older.

I don't think it was that night at the ballpark, but somewhere around that time a big idea came into my head, about the difference between mothers and fathers, and why you need one of each, if possible. Moms, being grown up and very practical — most of them — will help you start your own bank account so you can save up for that new twenty-four-speed bicycle you want to get. Dads, not quite as practical and still part boy — some of them — will help you build a spaceship bound for Mars.

29. The mystery of time more completely explained

The other night I saw a guy on TV who looked a lot like I do. It was like three in the morning and I couldn't sleep so I went downstairs and turned on the television and caught the end of an old science fiction movie called *Blade Runner*, starring Harrison Ford. It looked like it was an R-rated film but oh well, I can get away with a lot these days, too much. Anyway, Harrison Ford was fighting a dying white-haired replicant named Roy, a kind of android. Right before he ran out of life, Roy said, "I've seen things you people wouldn't believe. Attack ships on fire off the shoulder of Orion. I watched C-beams glitter in the dark near Tannhäuser Gate. All those moments will be lost in time, like tears in rain." Cool quote, huh, and deep?

As far as looks go, Roy the replicant and I could be cousins.

See the similarities? And listen to what Roy said: Time is a thief. The worst kind. It takes everything.

These days I hardly ever wear a wristwatch, and I try not to look at any clocks when I'm at school or at home. What's the point? I already know that time is out of control, keeps rolling along like a boulder down a hill, even when we want it to stop and take a rest. Or to turn back and replay the past, if only for one day. Just look at me, a victim of time. Not so long ago I didn't even exist. Then I was a seed and an egg that decided to join forces, then a fetus the size of a quarter, then a bigger fetus the size of a grapefruit, then an even larger fetus, able to suck a thumb inside my safe little womb. Go Finn the Amazing Fetus!

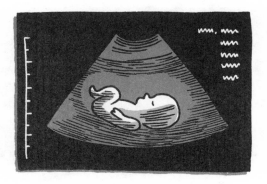

The first ever picture of me

Time kept marching along and I was born, tossed into the world, and became a baby, then a toddler, then a little kid, and then a bigger kid, and then me, who I am today, this minute, on my way to becoming an adult, visible or invisible, whether I like it or not.

And time will keep sprinting forward like a kid made hyper by too much sugar, and I'll be in my twenties, then thirties, then middle age, then old age. Maybe I'll even be a grandfather, or a wise but lonely old man, living by himself in a mountain cave. Need to hear something smart? Come see me.

And then I will stop but time will go on. And then maybe I'll come back and do it all over again, as a walrus or a fig tree or a laptop computer, or as the boy who saves the world.

It's the same story for my mom, my brother, my cat, for every living thing. It was the same story for my dad. They were nothing and then they were something. They were small and then they got bigger, all due to time.

And time tears us up and then it tries to fix us.

And time is a one-way street, even if we want it to be a two-way street.

And that is everything I know about time.

Ticktock, ticktock, ticktock . . .

30. The log of the Starship Finn Garrett, entry V

EARTH DAY SEPTEMBER 30, 1:41 P.M. The Reds' season ends today. They are on TV right now, Reds versus Cubs, but Derek and I aren't watching the game and it's not because the Reds won't make the playoffs for the millionth year in a row. It's just too hard, to watch the games without Dad there with us, cheering and acting silly. That was our summer weekend thing that we all loved.

Instead, my brother and I are watching a SpongeBob marathon on Nickelodeon. We've seen all of these episodes before, but Derek laughs anyway, like the jokes are new. Sometimes even I laugh. That happens.

Mom? Last I knew she was in her room, finally answering all of the sympathy cards and letters that swamped us in June. A hundred people saying sorry, sorry, sorry.

Life as we know it, at 1338 Columbus Avenue, Sunnyvale, Ohio.

3:50 P.M. Walk by Mom's room. Hear her crying in there, in the sniffling and groaning kind of way. Wonder if I should say something. Wonder if I should do something. Decide that it's too much for me to deal with. I walk away. Go outside and catch some sunshine.

What would you have done?

31. A true story about a vanishing boy, part IV

I keep disappearing, getting paler and paler. A living whiteout I'm becoming, the Human Snowstorm. Hair, skin, eyebrows, *me*, all losing their color. The pale knows why. I trust it. Sort of.

But I'm not totally white and black, there is some color left. My eyes, those rebels, refuse to be erased, are still ocean blue, look like blue dots painted on the black-and-white photograph that is me. *Let's add some color to this kid, modernize him.* And my chubby tongue is the normal shade of pink, and my lips still look like normal boy lips. Normal boy lips pasted on a pasty freak.

Eyes are pretty weird, don't you think? They *see* things.

The trillion colors. The trillion things to see. Like this book, like these words, like the white spaces around the words. If you think too much about how your eyes work, how they pull the world inside of you, you may get a severe case of the thinking ooglies.

A rest stop, in case you just got the thinking ooglies.

32. When words go wild

You are like I was, when I was me. I used to read a lot, about everything: dogs, outer space, corny stories involving pirates, biographies of famous people, graphic novels about superheroes and normal people trying to live super lives, and an anime series about a cheerleader-detective named Nikki Zero who solved all of the crimes and mysteries going on at her high school. Nikki, in case you want to know, means "victory of the people."

I'd spend hours at the library and the downtown bookstore, checking out the new books—even crime and suspense novels meant for adults and picture books meant for little kids—and the not-so-new books on the shelves, and books that were so old the binding glue was failing and the pages were brittle. I loved reading, and just about every librarian and bookstore employee in Sunnyvale knew me by name. *There's Finn again, losing himself in books. Hello, Finn!*

But now words jump and twist and flip and try to make themselves into different words. *E*'s and *a*'s slip and slide, are out of control. *W*'s think they're *M*'s. *T*'s insist they are *I*'s, while *p*'s flip up and pretend they are *b*'s, then flip sideways and become *d*'s. It doesn't make for easy reading when vowels and consonants do as they please.

Typing on my computer or on the ones at school can also be a nightmare, my scrambled brain believing that the word "books" is really spelled "koobs," and so on and so on (or "adn os no adn os no"). It took a good hour just to get these couple pages right, typing what I wanted to say, then making all of the corrections, then correcting the corrections that were incorrect, and then doing that again. But I will not give up. This is my story and I need to tell it before I go totally transparent. In the meantime my computer spell-check program is thinking of suing me for a million counts of software abuse.

My self-diagnosis? Dyslexia plus ADD plus ADHD plus FBID (Freak Boy Invisibility Disorder). The cure? Unknown.

33. Floodwaters

When you lose your dad just about anything can set off a flood of tears and memories. Like the time I found a pocket comb my dad used to use, a few of his hairs stuck in it. I could have cried for a week. Or the time I answered the phone and was certain I heard my dad's voice saying, "How's it going, little man?" but it turned out to be my stupid uncle Jacob. Or sometimes even just a jet, flying over my house, can ruin my day.

It happened again this morning. I was sitting in the living room and flipping through the newspaper, making my way to the sports section and then the funnies, when I saw a full-page ad for the sporting goods store my dad used to manage, World Champ Sports. Instantly, I was sobbing like a nutcase, which made no sense at all. We have stuff all over the house—coffee cups, Frisbees, baseball caps—that says WORLD CHAMP SPORTS on it. But seeing that ad just blew me away.

I ran upstairs to my room and cried and thought about my dad and his job. At least once a month Mom would take my brother and me to the mall, to visit Dad at the store. We usually saw him before he saw us. He might be helping a kid find a pair of soccer shin guards, or telling an old guy about the different brands of golf clubs they sold, or setting a tray of money inside a cash register. Dad liked to complain about his job, but most times when we were there he seemed to be a cheerful guy. And he was always happy to see his wife and kids trooping into the store. "There's my better three fourths," he'd sometimes say.

There were some privileges from being the manager's kid. Derek and I could hang out behind the counter where customers weren't allowed, putt plastic golf balls down the aisles as long as the store wasn't too busy, play foosball and Nerf basketball in the stockroom, and Dad would buy us whatever we wanted from the vending machines in the employee break room. "On the house," he'd say, like we were junior royalty. Visiting Dad at the store, even during the crazy summer and holiday sales, was always a ton of fun.

But now it's a different world we are living in. The few times we've gone to the mall since The Terrible Day That Changed Everything, my mom and brother and I totally avoid the wing of the mall where World Champ Sports sits. I'm not sure who's managing that store now, but it isn't my dad.

Anyway, I kept crying, thinking about my dad and his dumb store, until I ran out of tears. I dried my face with a towel and hurried downstairs and hunted around for my backpack, then caught the school bus and tried to get through my day, hoping that a fresh supply of tears didn't suddenly show up. All because of a stupid newspaper ad.

Here's something I know. I'd give the whole world, if I owned the whole world, for one more visit with my dad at his store, or anywhere. I'd give the galaxy. I'd give the entire gigantic universe.

34. Love notes

Gray afternoon. Riding bikes with Melanie, to her basketball practice at the middle school. Side by side, so cars have to go way around us. Meli is wearing her shiny silver and blue uniform, number 22. I'm in a sweatshirt and jeans and am currently unnumbered.

"You are the talk of the town," Meli says, as we pedal along. "Everyone is wondering what's going on with you."

"Really?" I say. "What are they saying?"

She: "Anything you can imagine."

Me: "Like 'What a handsome, fun, and smart kid. I wish I were him'?"

She: "Not so much that. It's more like 'Why is Finn's hair so white these days, and why is he so pale?' They're worried about you."

Me: "That's cool."

She: "Have you figured anything out? It's not a disease, right?"

Me: "Don't think it is. I feel pretty good. My doctor hasn't found anything."

She: "Something with your dad, then? The thing that happened."

Me: "Yeah, probably that."

She: "Guess it will work itself out, in time. Right?"

Me: "Guess so. Hope so."

A few blocks from the school, now.

Meli: "Some girls are like 'Why are you even hanging out with that kid? He's getting weirder looking every day.'"

Me: "Which girls?"

She: "Just a few girls. Why?"

Me: "From the team?"

She: "Maybe."

I hate it when people try to mess up our friendship. They should leave Meli and me alone, mind their own business. Actually it's just two of Meli's friends from the basketball team, Valerie Grant and Nora Holmes, who are causing all of the trouble. They want to fix Meli up with a dumb jock seventh grader named Reece Braverman, even though Meli has told them she's not ready to date anyone, and when she is ready, Finn Garrett, that's me, will be the lucky guy, even though I'm not even close to being a jock. *Finn can lift a can of green beans with a single hand!* Valerie means "to be strong," and Nora means "honor"—more names that don't fit—while Reece is a Welsh name that means "enthusiasm." Not sure if Reece is an enthusiastic guy. I hardly know the kid.

She: "Are you mad? Don't be mad. It's not like I care what other people think."

Me: "Not mad. Some of my friends are like 'Why are you always with Melanie? She is so much cooler than you.'" The truth? What Ben and my few other friends usually say about me hanging out with Meli is, "Sweet!"

She: "I'm cooler than you? Really?"

Me: "By a million miles."

She: "That's flattering, but I'd rather be happy than cool."

Smiles.

———

Across from the school we stop our bikes near what some kids call Make-out Woods, but for Meli and me it's more Hold Hands and Make Goofy Eyes at Each Other Woods. Or sometimes I just listen to Melanie complain about her mean dad and her dumb mom, who lives in Boulder, Colorado. Her mom hardly ever phones Melanie or even writes or sends e-mails, and she only flies Meli out to see her for two weeks every summer. Her parents both stink. Her dad is too involved in Meli's life. Her mom not nearly enough.

We hop off of our bikes and march to our favorite spot, a clearing in the middle of the woods, crunching a whole bunch of fallen leaves along the way. Meli looks at me, then grins big and closes her eyes and does something different—she kisses me on the cheek. Weirdly, it feels like she just pushed a diamond into my face, like that part of me is shiny and glowing and worth a million bucks.

"What was that for?" I dumbly ask.

"It's medicine," Meli says, glowing her own diamondy light. "Maybe it will save you."

"Thanks," I brilliantly say.

And then Meli pulls away, has to get to practice. If she's late, Coach Zeleski will make her run laps. "See you, Whitey," she says, walking toward our bikes.

"Not if I see you first," I say, still feeling a little dazed.

I stay standing in the quiet woods for a minute, just me and the birds and the trees, then I tramp to my mountain bike and ride home, to write down all of these words before I forget them.

Today's big lesson: Even half-invisible freak kids can be knocked silly by sudden love.

35. The log of the Starship Finn Garrett, entry VI

EARTH DAY OCTOBER 2, 5:18 P.M. Working on the Love Notes chapter and wondering what Dad would think about me wanting to someday marry Melanie. He knew Meli pretty well, sometimes tossed a football to both of us, drove us places like the lake and the library, but he didn't know that I liked her in the mushy kind of way. I wonder what he would think. What father-to-son advice he might have to offer if he were still around. Maybe, *Always treat girls with respect,* or something corny like that.

Want to go somewhere with me? It's about a mile from here. The place we are traveling to, it's not for everyone. Ready?

36. Cemetery Tales I

*If you see a boy sitting alone on a hill at the Green Oaks
Cemetery in Sunnyvale, Ohio, chances are it's me.*

This is where my father lives now. His bones, not his
soul. His soul is in heaven or is out buzzing around
the universe, or maybe he's already begun his next life.
Could be a baby sea lion or a NASA space probe about
to be launched to Jupiter or a curly blue fern living deep
in a South American rain forest. I kind of hope he's still

buzzing around. Dad loved to buzz around, in cars and on his motorcycle and on his mountain bike.

"Nothing like the feeling of wind in your hair," Dad used to say when he and I would ride together on his old Harley-Davidson motorcycle. I'd wrap around my father and hold on for dear life, even though we always rode under the speed limit, and usually just up and down the quiet streets in our neighborhood. I always wore a helmet, and Dad did too when we rode together, but sometimes when he took off on his own he'd leave his helmet at home, which always upset Mom and I didn't like it much either: Why take such a stupid risk? Testing himself, I guess. I loved our rides together, just Dad and me. In my head I can still hear the mighty Harley *vroom*s as my father cycled through the engine, the world streaking by.

Where's the Harley now? Mom sold it to Uncle Jacob for $800. She said we needed the cash, but I think she was worried that Derek and I would want to ride it when we got older. Mom isn't a big fan of motorcycles.

"Nothing like the open highway," Dad used to say when he'd take my mom and my brother and me on long drives, sometimes in the SMV but more often in his Chrysler. Usually on Friday or Saturday nights, a couple times each month during the spring, summer, and fall, and now and then during the winter when the weather was decent. One cool thing, we never knew where we were going until we got there—Dad kept us guessing. Could be farmland or a forest or a big city, like Columbus or Dayton, just to see the tall buildings and mega shopping centers and the busy lives of the people who lived there. No matter where we traveled to, on the way home we'd almost always stop somewhere for root beer floats or ice cream cones if it was summer, or warm apple cider or hot chocolate if it was winter.

We still own the Chrysler, it's parked in the driveway. Mom is keeping it around in case the SMV breaks down, but I'm hoping it will be my car in a few years. In Ohio you can get a driver's license when you turn sixteen.

"Nothing like getting away from it all," Dad would say as he and Derek and I, and sometimes Mom, would ride our bicycles down winding dirt trails in the Chauncey County Nature Preserve or the paved trails in the Big Pines State Forest, twenty miles southwest of Sunnyvale. Some of the times when we were in the forest we would

stop our bikes and pick wild black raspberries or elder-
berries that grew alongside the paths, and then later Mom
would make a cobbler or a berry pie, Derek and I helping
out. Or my brother and I would go hunting for rocks and
pinecones and shed bird feathers, especially from cardinals
and blue jays.

Dad's mountain bike is in the garage, hanging upside
down from the ceiling like a giant bat. It will become my
bike when I grow a few inches taller, and then Derek will
get my current bike, if it hasn't fallen apart, and we'll sell
his bicycle at a garage sale or donate it to Goodwill.

Why all of the running around like crazed chickens?
Dad said he was born with ants in his pants. Tough for
him to sit still. He always wanted to be going somewhere,
doing something, seeing the world. Some nights he even
had trouble sleeping, not wanting to waste seven or eight
hours on something as boring and "nonproductive" as sleep.
Like Dad I also have ants in my pants, but unlike him I'm

a big fan of sleep. Could go twelve hours a night if I could get away with it. Mom once said that if sleep were a sport then Finn Garrett would be the world champ. At least I used to be that way. Nowadays I often wake up five, six times each night, like there's something I need to urgently do, but I have no idea what. I'll fight to get back to sleep, only to wake up again an hour later, feeling like there are huge, planet-saving things I should be doing. It totally sucks. And when I can't sleep at all, which happened last night, and two nights before that, I'll go downstairs and watch old movies on TV, or bug Henry the cat, or I'll work on this book.

About the only kind of travel my father didn't like much was by Rollerblade or ice skate. The first time Dad tried Rollerblades he had a bad wipeout on the sidewalk in front of our house—his feet went flying out from under him and he bruised his tailbone. "If God had meant us to have wheels on our feet he would have put them there," he said a few minutes later, searching the linen closet for the heating pad. And whenever Derek and I and sometimes Mom went ice-skating at the rink in Ashton City, Dad would watch from the benches on the sidelines. "If God had meant for us to have blades on our feet . . ."

Want to hear something kind of weird? Most of the time I feel extra alive when I'm here at the cemetery, like I have blood running through my veins instead of the usual peanut butter and jelly. Maybe it's because, unlike my Dad and all of the rest of the dead people, I'm free to leave here. Can jump up and down. Do somersaults. Shout, *Spotted tree monkeys!* if I wanted to. Bicycle home.

I'm alive, they aren't. I can write this, they can't. Sad for them. Happy for me. Weird, huh?

37. Cemetery Tales II

The graveyard is peaceful and pretty. An owl lives in one of the trees. He watches the world.

Dad is buried over there in a flat stretch of the cemetery, between graves for someone named Sheri V. Cashman and someone named Minerva Rodriguez. Sheri is from a French word that means "darling," and Minerva was the Roman goddess of wisdom and war. Dad would probably think that was pretty cool, being squeezed between two women for all of eternity.

I like to sit up here, on top of the hill, the highest point of my city. The crest, the zenith—yeah, I know how to use a thesaurus. I can see most of Sunnyvale from this spot, including my school and my house, beyond all of those trees. I sometimes feel like I'm an angel, a spirit kid, whose job it is to keep the dead company, watch over them and provide some updates about life. Sports scores and the latest news, maybe some jokes I heard. Some days I'm the only friend the dead have — there's no one here but me. Call me Cemetery Boy, friend of all souls who have passed on to the next world, and their left-behind bones.

Jeez, no wonder I'm turning bleachy white. White bones, white cemetery stones, white statues. This dead place is rubbing off on me.

A rest stop while I think deeply about that.

I visit the cemetery nearly every day, even when it's raining or when it's one of those gray, sinking days where something as simple as pedaling my bike seems like a huge chore. Rain is just the way to make green things grow, so I don't mind getting wet, maybe I'll grow too. It's not the tears of God, like I read on a sympathy card that was mailed to our house, don't ever think that. *Every time it rains, know that God is crying with you,* said the card. Hog feathers! (one of my dad's phrases). God may cry, but that's not what rain is. Rain is a good, lifey thing. Just ask anything green.

And when it's winter and snow begins to pile up I will walk here, or borrow some cross-country skis, or maybe Melanie will pull me to Green Oaks on a sled. She's strong enough to do that, nearly always crushes me at arm wrestling. *Mush, Meli, mush,* I will say, cracking an imaginary whip. Or I'll pull Meli on the sled, or even Derek if he wants to come out here, but he probably won't want to because he hates this place.

Why am I at Green Oaks so much? Have I gone loopy? Yes, I have gone loopy, but the real reason is this: Like how it was before The Terrible Day That Changed Everything, I want to hang out with my father as much as possible. Every day, or close to it. I really loved that guy.

38. Cemetery Tales III

My friend Benjamin came out to Green Oaks once but he only stayed like three minutes. The cemetery was giving him the willies, he said, the absolute creeps, so he quickly left. What a baby. I hardly ever get the willies here, but I do often get the saddies. I drip my tears onto the hill and help the grass to grow.

And sometimes Melanie and I will ride our bikes out here, she on her red Schwinn racer and me on my blue Raleigh mountain bike. We usually stop our bikes at the bottom of the cemetery hill and leave them there, or walk them to the top of the hill so later on we can race downhill, weaving between markers. That's always the weirdest kind of thrill.

Meli and I will usually sit together on the hill for an hour or longer, holding hands or not holding hands and saying next to nothing. We always try to be pretty serious and well behaved, since we are at a cemetery, but now and then some fun will break out. Like one time when we were sitting on a flat patch of land we started tickling each other, and that led to a wrestling match. Melanie pinned me to the grass for a two-count, then I bucked her off and tackled her and pinned her for a one-count, and then she kicked me off of her and pinned me for a three-count. Meli even did that gross thing where she dripped a string of drool from her mouth and just as it was about to splash me in the face and oogle me out forever, she slurped it back up.

But then we both remembered that we were having fun in a place where no one else was allowed to have fun, since they were dead, and Meli jumped off of me and I sat up, and for the rest of our stay at the cemetery we remained very serious and quiet. We didn't want to wake the dead or make God mad.

And one day Meli and I wandered into the graveyard meadow and got lost, but that's its own story.

Love in the Graveyard, by Finn Garrett

My friend Melanie and I had spent much of the early summer riding our bikes out to Green Oaks Cemetery, where my dad and hundreds of people I never met while they were still living are buried. But then, right after the Fourth of July, she left for a family vacation in North Carolina, and after that she spent two long weeks at a girls' basketball camp in Michigan. I didn't see her again until early August. On her first full day back we rode out to the cemetery and ended up getting lost in a meadow.

It was a sticky hot day. After spending a few minutes in a shady spot on the cemetery hill, gazing at our little town, Meli and I decided to check out the meadow on the south side of the graveyard. We had to cross a footbridge over a narrow creek to get there. The flowers and weeds in the meadow were "as tall as September corn," a phrase I heard my grandpa Victor use once or twice. Melanie and I were soon surrounded by different kinds of sun-colored flowers—brown-eyed Susans, goldenrod, wild sunflowers—and by other flowers and weeds we didn't know the names of, except for thistle. Monarchs and white moths and tiny black butterflies fluttered from flower to flower, and a fat queen bee buzzed by and scared us.

Our plan was to exit the meadow where we entered it, but we had wandered through it without leaving any bread crumbs or trails. "Where to?" Meli said, looking into the army of stalks and stems. "Let's try that way," I said, pointing to my right. Melanie and I moved through the meadow, sometimes walking, other times running, knocking aside tall flowers and avoiding plants that looked prickly. We came to a section of wild grass, stopped, looked around, then ran again, holding hands now and picking up the pace as we dashed through more tangles of flowers, and finally we found our way out. We were back at the cemetery side, maybe a hundred yards west of where we had entered the meadow. We stepped cautiously on creek stones to cross the water.

Melanie dropped down on the grass and I did the same. There was a long scratch on her right arm that looked like a string of hyphens, and burrs clung to her clothing. Meli moved closer to me and looked into my eyes, and I had this sudden weird feeling of being so totally in love that I wanted to scream. I don't think it was the boy-girl, Romeo-and-Juliet stuff, or at least it wasn't only that. It was like I was in love with who Meli *is*, not just what she looked like or what she said or did.

"You're looking pretty weirded out," she said. "Even more than usual."

There was a logjam of words in my head, but none of them seemed to be making their way to my mouth. But then I said to Meli, "You're cool."

"That's true," she said, smiling.

Meli then pulled burrs from my hair and clothes, and I pulled them from her hair and clothes. "Cockleburs are amazing," she said, watching me yank a burr from her basketball camp T-shirt. "How do weeds know that people and rabbits exist that they can attach their burrs to? Where are their eyes? Their brains? I think that's the biggest, most important question ever in the whole universe. How do they know?"

I didn't have any kind of answer and wished that I were a whole lot smarter than I was. A specialist in cocklebur biology.

We stood up and went and visited my dad's grave for a few minutes, just hung out and didn't say much, then we wandered to the old part of the cemetery, to visit with the Stanislov kids, whose three bodies rest below gravestones instead of markers, near a gnarled oak tree. Not one of the children made it to their tenth birthday, all dying between 1929 and 1942: Alice, Paul Jr., and Prue. Some hideous disease that has since been wiped out must have claimed them all, Melanie and I guessed. Book-sized stones, whitened by time, marked the little lives of the Stanislov kids. But where were the sad parents?

"Arctic scientists living in a land where nothing grows," Melanie said. "Their hearts are black, charcoal really, but somehow keep ticking."

"Good one," I said. Meli and I often made up imaginary lives for the dead and for their next of kin.

"Race you to the bikes," she then said. So we ran to our bicycles and walked them up the hill. We caught our breaths then jumped onto our bikes and coasted down the hill, weaving between the markers, once again daring the long dead, maybe Linda Bowers (passed in 1982), maybe Buck Hamilton (dead since 1994), to arise from their graves and shout, *You crazy kids!*

I wrote that story a few weeks ago, when I was still a refugee from Sunnyvale Middle. Did you like it, or not? For those keeping track, Linda is a Spanish word that means "beautiful," and a buck is a male deer. Alice means "noble type," Paul means "humble," and Prue means "good judgment."

Now that Melanie has basketball practice and games and lots of homework, she can only come out to the cemetery with me maybe once a week. I sure loved it when it was an everyday adventure, riding our bikes to Green Oaks in sunshine or in the rain. It can get a little lonely, out here on my own.

Jeez, I'm starting to creep myself out here, with all of this talk of life and death and bones and cemeteries. You too? Another rest stop while we de-creep ourselves.

39. Cemetery Tales IV

A few months ago, when I first started hanging out here, this hill was dotted with a billion tiny blue and white flowers. But they went away and hundreds of dandelions popped up. Then they went to seed and were soon gone, but then a second batch showed up, and now almost all of them have gone to seed and have disappeared, but a few of the puffballs remain. I've been tempted to blow on the seed puffs or kick them free but have to stop myself. If you send seeds places you better make sure they all find a home. It's a huge responsibility. And this means you too, wind! No more sending dandelion seeds onto roads or parking lots or roofs, or into lakes and creeks — I hate to see that. You can do better.

Have you noticed that many of the leaves on the graveyard trees are turning shades of orange and yellow and red and purple? All of those pretty colors — that's not death, it's life. The trees are closing up shop for the winter, shedding this year's batch of leaves. They'll be back in the spring.

We come here as a family, Mom and Derek and me, and sometimes Grandpa Victor, every week or two. The last time was this past Sunday. We brought fresh flowers—store-bought daisies—and Mom put them in the vase that is part of the marker and poured in water from a gallon jug. Vic then stooped and brushed fallen leaves and cut grass from the marker, like he always does when he's with us.

"Time to go," Derek said after we had been here for about a minute, but it was too soon to leave so we all stood around for another ten minutes, kicking at the grass and thinking our thoughts and not saying anything important. There's a driving range next to the cemetery, so Derek and I sometimes watched men and women and kids whack at golf balls with their clubs. One of the red-striped balls landed in the cemetery, so my brother went running after it, happy for something to do. He looked like he was thinking of keeping the ball, but then he threw it over the fence. Some lady on the other side of the fence said, "Thanks, sport." And then we left Green Oaks, the ride home dumb and disappointing. We keep leaving Dad at the cemetery. We never take him home with us.

I'd much rather be here by myself. I can talk to Dad, pray, cry, scream, or do nothing at all. Whatever I want or don't want. The cemetery is one of those few places in the galaxy where I don't have to pretend, don't have to act like I'm happy if I'm feeling sad. The dead, I've found out, are totally nonjudgmental.

I usually hop on my bike as soon as I get home from school, after I check in with Mom. Say hey if she's at home, or phone her at the bank. Not sure how Mom feels about me spending so much time at Green Oaks, but one time she said, "Don't love that place too much." I promised that I wouldn't.

My bike is pretty reliable—I only once got a flat and had to walk it home—but it has more speeds than I know what to do with. Dad tightened the chain, replaced the brake pads, installed extra reflectors. He was a good dad.

40. Cemetery Tales V

If you spend lots of your life at a cemetery you will meet all kinds of people, like beefy landscapers and gravediggers and slick funeral home people, but mostly you will meet people who have lost someone they love. Like George, a wrinkled old guy who, a few months ago, buried his wife that he was married to for thirty-nine years. "Margaret was the spice of my life," he said to me droopily. George, in case you are dying to know, means "earth worker" or "farmer," and Margaret means "pearl." A farmer found his pearl and then lost it.

And I met two blond-haired twin sisters in their thirties who lost their younger brother due to the Iraq War. Corporal Addison (his name means "son of Adam") Kent is buried at the bottom of the hill. The sunny side. His grave always has fresh carnations and a tiny American flag. And I met a family of seven who was visiting the grave of a woman named Beverly Fitzsimmons, mother to two of them, grandmother to four of them, and great-grandmother to one of them, the baby. Beverly means "beaver stream." No lie. It's a pretty-sounding name, but I'm not sure when or why some people started naming their daughters after a beaver stream.

Sometimes I tell visitors to Green Oaks about my dad, and sometimes I say I'm only here because I like the view, and other times I keep quiet. Once, I froze myself and pretended to be a statue of a boy sitting on the hill—I'm stone white enough that I can get away with the concrete look. I stayed that way for nearly a half hour. My nose itched like crazy but I didn't scratch it until all of the visitors had left. None of them gave me a second look. I kind of liked that, being unnoticed and left alone, even though I was very much here. And sometimes I wear my Reds baseball cap pulled low so no one will ask about my funky hair, and clothes that cover every inch of my arms and legs so no one will ask about my pasty skin. And sometimes I don't bother to hide my growing invisibility. Call me Morfinn Garrett, The Last Invisible Boy. (Get it, Morfinn sounds like the word "morphing"? Sorry.)

But right now, this minute that will soon be gone, I'm here with you, writing these words in my notebook and drawing some pictures. Just me and you and the grass and the trees and the three hundred dead people and the squirrels and the birds and that owl and the slightly tilted cemetery worker's shack that will one day fall down and the statue of Jesus near the cemetery gates and the one of the Virgin Mary in the old part of the cemetery. Thanks for staying so long with me in this weird little place.

41. Cemetery Tales VI

It's time. Let me take you somewhere. Ready?
Let's go.
Over here.
This way.
Just a little farther.
Come on.
A few more steps.
And now we are finally there.
This is where my dad is buried.

ALBERT RICHARD GARRETT

Do you like the coppery roses on the marker? I do.
Richard, my father's middle name, means "brave power."
Perfect.

I think I'll just sit here for a little while. Think about
stuff. You are welcome to stay, if you like. Or go.

42. Cemetery Tales VII

The next time you pass by a cemetery, holding your breath so you don't suck in demon spirits or zombie vapors, please remember this: Everyone buried there has a huge and important story to tell, the story of their life. They all started out as babies and went in a million different directions. Some became fathers or mothers, or were bachelors or old maids. They were athletes and wimps, scientists and dumbos, soldiers and hippies, priests and sinners, and each one had a big and mysterious and beautiful life, whether it lasted twenty years or a hundred years. And each of them had people, three or three hundred, who loved them and missed them when they were gone. And none of the dead can share their stories anymore so it's up to us to tell those stories or remember them or imagine them. I have named myself the keeper of my father's stories. Whose stories are you guarding?

The sun is beaming, just above the changing trees. It must be six, or half past. I better be riding home now, dinner should be ready. Spaghetti with turkey meatballs and the usual salad. Derek will try to roll a giant ball of spaghetti onto his fork. Mom will ask about my day. I'll tell her some things and leave out other things. Henry will walk around while we eat, hoping for some scraps or dropped noodles. And I'll be thinking about what to tell you next.

Today's confession: I'm happy to be alive.

43. The log of the Starship Finn Garrett, entry VII

EARTH DAY OCTOBER 8, 8:05 P.M. Derek is downstairs, watching SpongeBob, and hoping for a new episode involving Sandy the squirrel. I'm in the upstairs hallway, sitting on the thick carpet and working on some drawings for this book. Henry the cat is curled up near me, snoozing. Mom is in her room, crying old tears she kept buried inside or new tears she just made. She wears a brave face most of the time, but she can't keep wearing that mask forever. It will crack. It will fall off. Like that night she was doing laundry but suddenly went running into her room and stayed there the rest of the night. Derek and I ended up folding most of the clothes. Or like the night Mom told my brother and me to pack our suitcases because we were leaving for "a brand-new life very far away." We were most of the way packed before she canceled the plans.

Me, I'm wearing a pale face. A very pale face. Maybe only saltwater taffy can save me, restore my color and visibility. Time for my daily dose.

8:36 P.M. Mom is still crying in her room. I decide to do something this time. I knock on her door, ask if she wants to play Scrabble with Derek and me. Before The Terrible Day That Changed Everything we used to play Scrabble in teams, about once a week, usually Dad and me versus Mom and Derek, though really it was Mom versus Dad and my brother and I helped out a little and picked new letter tiles.

"You sure?" Mom says, clearing her throat and sniffling. "Because I'll kick your little butts."

"I'm sure," I say.

So we play Scrabble on the living room floor, Mom against Derek and me. Mom acts a little dumb so she won't blow us away, going with simple words like "reed" and "coal" and not using as many double- and triple-word bonus squares as she normally would. But since Derek and I are dumb for real, we don't have to pretend, Mom wins anyway, 158 to 92.

"Thanks for remembering me," Mom says as we are putting away the game.

I try to think of something brilliant and beautiful to say to my mother, but all I can come up with is, "Sure, Mom."

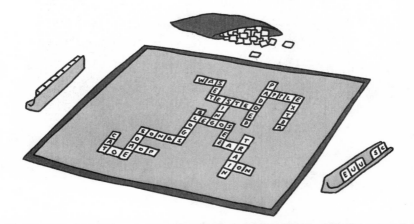

44. Derek's chapter

Note from Finn: I told my little brother that this chapter was his, that he could draw or write anything he wanted, about Dad or not about Dad. Derek came up with three drawings and a short essay he had to write for his fourth-grade teacher, Ms. Meyers, about this past summer. And then he gave me a red ribbon that he won last year for a school spelling contest. I wasn't exactly sure what to do with the ribbon, so the last drawing, of the ribbon, is by me.

See you in the next chapter.

Derek's drawings:

Me and my dad in outer space

What cats think about

Derek's words:

My Summer, by Derek Garrett

I hated this summer. I wish it never happened. It was the stupidest summer there ever was in the history of the world. I wish that it had gone straight from spring to winter, but it didn't. All of the time during the summer when I was asleep I dreamed it was snowing. Really big snowflakes. I wish it did snow, because then it would have been winter, not summer. I like winter, and the snow. But dreams hardly ever come true, except for some of the bad ones.

I also found lots of cool rocks with my brother Finn in the woods by the middle school and at Thompson Lake. And my mom grew tomatoes in pots, the small kind of tomato you put in salads, and I was the one who picked most of them. Those were the only good parts of the summer.

The end.

Note from Finn: Derek got a B- for his paper, and his teacher wrote, "I know it was a rough one, sorry. Next time try to write a little bit more."

Derek's prize:

Unexpected bonus material:

Note from Finn: Derek just asked me to show you some of the rocks he found this past summer. Here is my drawing of a few of them. Sorry we couldn't squeeze the real rocks into this book.

45. A true story about a vanishing boy, part V

I woke up today with pure white hair. Not old hair, not dead hair, just white hair. Not a single black strand anywhere in that messy white forest on my head. Not one! A freak yesterday, the King of Freaks today. And my skin was as white as new computer paper, the expensive stuff. As white as eggshells. Darn it, I'm almost out of here. Poof! But I'm not ready to be out of here.

I stumbled downstairs, worried that this was my last day or week or month as a visible kid, my new life as ghostly blur just about here. Booted from the world of the seeable and never to return. *Later, Finn, it was nice to SEE you. Ha!*

Mom's eyes doubled in size when she saw me, and she grabbed my wrist to feel for a pulse. My pulse beat strong. *K-thud, k-thud, k-thud.* And then Mom put a fleshy hand to my pale forehead but found no fever.

"Are you feeling okay?" she said. "Tell me what you need."

"Umm, breakfast maybe?" I said.

So we all ate breakfast. Waffles with strawberry syrup and a quarter stalk of celery filled with organic peanut butter. A few celery strings got caught in my teeth and I had to pull them out. I hate that. Mom kept looking at my Albert Einstein-like hair and Derek checked it out a few times and even Henry the cat was paying more attention to me than she usually does.

"I like your hair," Derek said, chomping at celery, his mouth sticky with peanut butter.

"Thanks," I said.

"Don't encourage him," Mom said to Derek. What? Mom thinks I'm turning my hair white, making myself invisible so I can what, hang out with Dad? Or slay sleeping Gorgons like Perseus? Maybe Mom's right, but if I do own such awesome powers why don't I make my hair blue and my skin red? Or my hair dark green and my skin light green, a not-so-Incredible Hulk? Or even go with scaly lizard skin and a forked tongue?

About an hour after breakfast Mom took me to see Dr. Patel, our family doctor. This was the fifth or sixth time I've seen Dr. Patel for "the whiteness thing." He has yet to find a cause or a cure.

At the doctor's office we waited. And waited. And waited some more. And that's why they call it a waiting room.

46. The log of the Starship Finn Garrett, entry VIII

EARTH DAY OCTOBER 12, 9:37 A.M. Mom is reading an old *Ladies' Home Journal*. Beautiful house on the cover, nicer than ours. I'm writing these words. Oversize man with a bad cough comes into the waiting room. Looks at me like he's worried he'll catch my disease. Tells receptionist — *cough, cough* — that he'll be back "in a few," that he left something important in the car. The man glances at me again and scoots away. Receptionist looks at me like I just caused the end of the world. *Sorry.*

Dr. Patel opens the door. Says, "Hello again Finn and Finn's mother. Come in." He probably sees ten or twelve vanishing kids a day, I'm thinking. It's a terrible, world-wide epidemic.

I wish. It's only me. Have to go now.

47. Can you pass the exam?

I didn't tell Dr. Patel that I was turning invisible, that I was being slowly erased from the seeable world. I was afraid he'd lock me up in a hospital mental ward, or at least try to take pictures of my brain, to see if it has shrunk to the size of a prune or if maybe one of my replicant circuit boards has shorted out. But I don't wish to have my brain photographed, thank you very much. My brain, like the rest of me, is very camera shy.

Dr. Patel did the usual examination—told me to show my tongue, cough three times, took my temperature and blood pressure, tapped my knees with a stone hammer to make sure my reflexes weren't spazzy—then he stole enough blood from a vein in my left arm to fill a needle. I wanted the blood back. It's mine, I made it, give it back. My blood was still a color, tomato-sauce red. The doctor gave it to a nurse, to run some tests.

Mom and I waited in a consultation room for the results. Mom read a brochure about anxiety. I gazed at a model of the human lung and thought about my own spongy lungs, and other stuff. Mom rubbed my back in a "we'll get to the bottom of this" kind of way. I remembered that I was supposed to be worried about turning invisible.

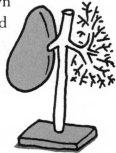

The doctor came back in, carrying a printout. "Good news," he said. "Finn remains perfectly normal and healthy." Yeah, Normal Boy, that's me. Used to be.

"But there has to be something wrong with him," Mom said to the doctor. "Kids just don't have hair that color, and they aren't *that* pale."

This kid does and is, I thought.

Said the doctor, "His iron level is good, CBC is fine, he has plenty of B_{12}, there's no evidence of an infection. As far as I can tell there is nothing medically wrong with Finn." He smiled at me. I forgot to smile back.

Said Mom, "Perhaps I should get a second opinion. We must be missing something. I mean, just look at him. That's not normal."

Said my head, *I'm here. I can hear you. Hello.*

Said the doctor, "Get as many opinions as you like, but blood doesn't lie."

Said my head, *Maybe some blood lies, like blood taken from a liar.*

Said Mom, "We have to get to the bottom of this. Don't you have any ideas at all? Crazy notions? Wild guesses?"

Dr. Patel gazed at me like he was studying a model of a human boy, looking for the part that was out of place. "It's possible," he said, "that Finn could be experiencing a healing crisis. Sometimes right before a person heals they briefly get a whole lot worse. I've seen this happen, from time to time, in some of my other patients."

So that's the explanation. I've been turning myself invisible so I can someday be fully visible again. Mystery solved!

"You really think that could be it?" Mom said. "That we

may soon be seeing the old Finn again?" She means the black-haired Finn who used to wear a dumb smile on his face most of the day. That kid left town in June and hasn't been seen since.

"We should know soon," Dr. Patel said. "Keep an eye on Finn, looking for signs of improvement."

And then we left Dr. Patel's office. He didn't offer me a lollipop. I used to get lollipops from Dr. Patel all of the time when I was little. Knowing that candy was waiting for me if I didn't cry and complain too much made the needle pain or the taste of icky medicines a little more bearable. Usually the choice was between a cherry lollipop or a grape lollipop, but sometimes the doctor only had cherry, too many kids going for the grape ones. You lose some great things when you start to grow up. Like free lollipops.

Here's a comic I drew. I hope you like it.

Doctor, Save My Child!

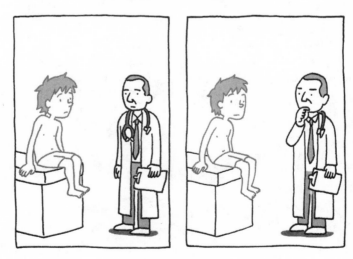

48. Welcome to the freak show, starring me

On the way to school I gazed at myself in the car mirror, the side one, glad I could still be seen, for now, by me and by the world. And I decided that I liked my hair in this color, whatever this color was called. China white? Eyeball white? Goose-feather white? It made me feel wise and witchy, the white hair, like Gandalf, that old guy from *Lord of the Rings*. Like Roy, the replicant from *Blade Runner*. It made me feel like a survivor.

As we pulled in front of Sunnyvale Middle, Mom said I could take a sick day if I wanted to, since I already missed four of my classes, but that sounded totally boring so I decided to go to school.

"Don't listen to the other kids," Mom said, right before I left her. "Who cares what they think of your appearance."

"I don't," I lied. And then I went and faced what I knew was coming. *Hey, everyone, look at the freak!*

In the hallway some kids pointed or gave me the Weird Eye, and one or two of them even laughed. So what? And this oatmeal-for-brains girl named Tabitha Carlson said, "Hello there, Old Man Garrett. Forget to bring your walker to school today?" That wasn't very nice, dissing both me and old people. I tried to think of the perfect comeback line, but all I could come up with was, *At least I'm not named after a wimpy animal (Tabitha means "gazelle" in Aramaic).* Sucky comeback, I know. Fortunately I didn't actually say that dumb thing to Tabitha and went on to my class. But before I got there I ran into Melanie.

"Holy cow!" she said, giving me the once-over. "You really turned it up a notch. Are you feeling okay?"

"My doctor says I'm fine," I said.

"Fine if you're the Pillsbury Doughboy," she said.

As Meli and I started walking, a big question I had kept locked down for weeks somehow escaped. "Will you still like me once I'm completely invisible?" I asked her.

Meli laughed. "You are not turning invisible. You are just very, very, very, very white."

"But if I was invisible, totally vanished, would you still want to be friends? I really need to know."

"You're not turning invisible!"

"But if I was . . ."

"You're not!"

We stopped at Meli's classroom. She scrunched her face then said, "We could still run around like idiots, if you were invisible? Even though that won't ever happen."

"I don't see why not," I said.

"In that case, sure, I'll still like you when you're invisible," she said. "Happy? Just don't sneak up on me and scare me. I hate that."

I promised Meli I wouldn't sneak up on her, and then she rolled her eyes and went inside her class, English, and I marched to my class, earth science. This pale little freak carried on.

49. Choosing sides

There are two kinds of kids in this world: the freaks and those who point out the freaks. Which kind of kid are you? Which kind do you want to be?

Of the freaks, there are the happy to be freaks and the unhappy to be freaks. I've decided to be in the first category. Freaks rule the world! Or they should. If you are in the second category, an unhappy freak, please come over to my side. I made lemonade.

50. Sudden freckles and missing graham crackers

Third meeting with Dr. Amanda. I'd much rather be at the cemetery.

"My, oh my," Dr. A says, gazing at my white hair and dull skin with her dark eyes. "What's going on with you, Finn?"

I shrug. She keeps looking and looking and looking. I could use some total invisibility about now.

"I once had a client," Dr. A says, "a woman in her sixties who had freckles bloom on her face, her arms, all over, after she lost her sister. This woman hadn't had freckles since she was a fourteen-year-old girl, but they were suddenly back again. I thought that perhaps in some symbolic way her body was trying to take her back to her childhood, to happier days."

"How'd she lose her sister?" I ask.

"Not sure. Does it matter?" she says.

"A little," I say.

"I think it was a rare form of cancer," she says. "But my point with you, with your hair and skin turning white like this, maybe your body, in a symbolic way, is taking you in the opposite direction, to your old age, so you are closer to your own ending. Closer to maybe seeing your father again. Make sense? I could be way off base here."

"Makes a little sense," I say. It is true that I want to know where Dad is at, in heaven or in a different dimension, or maybe back on Earth, living life in a new form. And I'd love to see him and hang out with him, wherever or whatever he is. Just me and my father, kicking around the universe.

"It's only a theory," Dr. Amanda says, "but everything is wired together, you know. Body, mind, and soul."

Something to think about when my head is working right again.

"One thing you can do," she says, "is to periodically remind yourself that it's okay to just be a kid. In fact, say those words to your body, ten or twenty times each day: 'It's okay to just be a kid.' Maybe that will help some."

"I'll try that," I say. And then, "Ever hear of a person turning invisible? I mean a real person. Not a character in a movie."

"I don't think that's physically possible," she says.

"Okay," I say.

"You think you're turning invisible, is that it?" she says. "I can see you quite clearly, Mr. Garrett. Maybe even more than most people."

"Okay," I say.

"You don't have to always agree with me," she says.

"Okay," I say.

Dr. A smiles then moves her eyes to the side, like she's doing some heavy thinking. "If you feel like you are invisible, or soon will be, I'd say, symbolically, that's pretty heavy stuff. Invisible people, if they existed, are of this world but not of this world. They are here, but you can't see them. Is that what you want, to be here but not be seen? Have the world all to yourself, in a way?"

"Sort of, but not really," I say, my brain starting to hurt from too much thinking. "I want to be in this world, but also the other one, where my dad's at. At the same time."

"Of course you do," Dr. Amanda says. "But I don't think that's possible. So I'd suggest—"

"I want my dad back," I blurt out, surprising myself. Tears leap to my eyes but I'm able to keep them from falling by pretending I'm a tough guy. Made of steel.

"Completely understandable," Dr. A says, smiling in a sympathetic kind of way. "We'd all like to change the ways of the world, if we could. Bring back loved ones, end all suffering. It's part of what makes us human, these gigantic wishes."

"I guess," I say.

While Dr. Amanda is gazing at me and maybe trying to come up with something smart to say, I take my notebook out of my backpack and write down what she just said and what I just said, before I lose the words.

"What are you writing there?" she asks.

"My first book," I say. "I'm thinking of becoming a writer. And maybe an artist."

"Go for it," Dr. A says, smiling so brightly that it's tough for me to stay bummed out and nervous. Smiles can unmess you up like that.

End of session. I ask for some graham crackers and a juice box.

"Sorry," she says, "I forgot to bring them today. My bad."

I'm only here for the graham crackers, I almost say but don't. Instead: "I thought they were the school's graham crackers and juice boxes."

She laughs. "The district is too cheap to pay for crackers and juice."

Now I know.

51. The log of the Starship Finn Garrett, entry IX

EARTH DAY OCTOBER 12, 4:10 P.M. Bicycling to Green Oaks. Stopped by a slow-moving train. Wonder where it's heading. Wonder if I'd be happy there. My dad probably loved trains. They can take you to places you've never been before.

"It's okay to just be a kid," I say to my body. Worth a try. *What's that, old man?* says my body. *Could you speak up? I'm hard of hearing.*

5:38 P.M. Home. Seemed like every eyeball at school and in Sunnyvale was aimed at me today, like I was a strange species of animal they had never seen before. *Homo sapiens invisibilus.* All of that staring is kind of weird, if you think about it. The less of me there is to see the more I get looked at. When I was completely visible hardly anyone noticed me. Now that I'm vanishing everyone sees me, like . . . like a star that goes supernova, shining brightly before disappearing from the sky. Or a lightbulb that scares you with a blast of light before burning out. Could this be the one true explanation for what's happening to me, that I'm burning bright white before blowing a fuse?

If I keep disappearing I will look like this:

And then this:

And then this:

I'll still be here but you won't be able to see me, unless you happen to own a pair of infrared goggles, or maybe X-ray glasses would do the trick. But I'll be able to see you and everything you do. So no picking your nose!

5:51 P.M. Check my reflection in the mirror. Wonder for the thousandth time what is going on. The weirdest case of adolescence ever? Consider running to the store and buying some hair dye meant for little old ladies, or Grecian Formula 16, and some girly makeup so my skin looks more human, less replicant. Nah. As the sweet potato likes to say, "I yam who I yam." A dumb joke my father used to tell.

Here are a few pictures of Dad and me:

This was taken at a water park called Wonder Wave.

*Right before my soccer game. Soccer is the only sport
I don't suck at due to my snappy legs. I was good at
stealing the ball, then kicking it a mile.*

My favorite photo of all time. I keep it close by.

7:15 P.M. In the kitchen, trying to find a snack I want to eat. The phone rings so I answer it.

"Could I speak with Mr. Garrett, please?" says some guy, probably a salesman. The zillionth time this has happened.

"He's not home," I say.

"Do you know when—"

I hang up. Mom comes into the room. "Who was on the phone?" she asks.

"Wrong number," I say.

Sometimes I hate my dad for leaving us.

8:42 P.M. Have to give Henry the cat a bath. This should be a sudsy mess.

52. Decision time

I know I haven't said much about what happened to my dad. Sorry. I've been putting it off for as long as possible because it's very sad. But maybe it's time? If you're ready to find out the Terrible Truth then go to the next chapter. If not, then set this book down and come back later. Or tomorrow. Or in three months. Or never (I won't be mad).

53. The next installment of The Terrible Truth

It was a June day crazy with sunlight. The call from the airline came at about three in the afternoon. Mom, Derek, and I were in the kitchen . . .

No, sorry. I'm not ready to do this yet. Come back next chapter.

54. The actual next installment of The Terrible Truth

It was a June day crazy with sunlight. The call from the airline came at about three in the afternoon. Mom, Derek, and I were in the kitchen, enjoying a healthy snack. Carrot sticks and pomegranate juice, I think it was. Mom was on a "let's get plenty of vitamins and antioxidants" kick at the time. She had worked a half day at the bank and was home, taking it easy with her lazy kids. Otherwise it might have been me, answering the phone. I'm glad it wasn't me.

Anyway, it was a pretty normal day. No school, nothing to do, let's have a snack. But normalcy was about to go flying out the window and it hasn't been seen here since. It left when Mom picked up the phone and then seemed to sink inside her own skin.

"Yes, this is his wife," Mom said, to whoever was on the phone.

"My God," Mom then said, to whoever was on the phone.

"You must be kidding me," Mom then said, to whoever was on the phone. "I just spoke with him a few hours ago. He was fine. Said he'd see us tonight."

"But there are Garretts all over the place," Mom then said, to whoever was on the phone. "You have the wrong family. Find the right one and give them the bad news."

"Oh," Mom then said, to whoever was on the phone.

"Yes, okay," Mom then said, to whoever was on the phone. "We'll be there."

And then Mom hung up. She looked half gone, like she had switched off her brain but her body was still working. "There's been a little trouble with your father," was all she said to my brother and me, not looking at us. Dad had been out of town for a few days, in Boston, visiting a friend, and was due home either later that day or the next day, I wasn't sure which. A "little trouble" could have meant that he caught a bad cold while in Boston or that maybe he somehow broke a pinky, like it got slammed in a car door. Those kinds of little things happen all of the time. But Mom's face wasn't saying "little trouble." Her face had gone ghost white, like how my skin is now.

For the next hour Derek and I dumbly sat at the table while Mom made a hundred phone calls, to relatives and to the airport and to some other people and places, always speaking really quietly, sparing my brother and me most of the details, I guess. But one thing was becoming clear: Dad wasn't going to be coming home.

"Albert's gone," Mom said to someone on the other end of the phone line. "They're saying he's gone. I just can't believe it. Tell me that it can't be true."

Whoever my mother was speaking with must not have told her the words she wanted to hear, because the next thing Mom did was place a hand over her eyes so Derek and I wouldn't see her cry. It didn't work too good, that hand shield. We saw her tears.

Later that afternoon, Mom, Derek, and I headed to the big airport in Columbus, picking up Grandpa Victor at his house in Newbury Falls along the way. Henry the cat stayed at home. It was the worst drive ever, Mom saying things like, "This has to be a terrible mistake," and Vic looking like he wanted to say a million things but not saying anything at all. Derek also stayed quiet during the hour-long drive. And I felt like a kid actor starring in a dumb movie about a boy who just lost his dad, unless the Mom actress was right and it all had been a terrible mistake. This was the stupid drive-to-the-airport scene that seemed to go on forever.

At the airport Mom parked the SMV in a lot and we took a shuttle bus to the main entrance. Most people outside and inside the terminal seemed to be having a normal day, were running to catch a plane or were hugging loved ones hello or good-bye. As far as I could tell my family and I were the only ones on the verge of a massive freak-out.

We somehow found our way to the right airline counter, Con-Tran Airways, then an airline employee, a lady with big red hair, took us to a back room where a different employee, a man with a pink, round face and thin blond hair—it looked like fake doll's hair—gave us gingersnaps and orange sodas while we waited for whatever we were waiting for. The man with the doll's hair stayed with us but was of absolutely no use. He was only there because someone told him to stay with us. I wanted to pinch him hard and pull his weird hair.

A terrible, twisting twenty minutes passed, then a brown-haired man wearing a light blue suit came into the room and said, "The plane is here." This pretty much eliminated any chance that there had been a crash or some kind of mechanical trouble with the plane, which I had nearly scratched off the list of "What Happened to Dad" possibilities anyway. If there had been a crash or if one of the engines had blown up, we wouldn't have been the only family waiting.

The man in the light blue suit motioned to my mom. She stood up weakly, like some kind of animal born with thin, wobbly legs, and went to him. For three or four minutes they spoke in quiet voices, Mom nodding a lot and the man looking concerned a lot. I only picked up a handful of the man's words, like "arrangements" and "paperwork" and "sorry."

Mom sat back down with us, and the man in the light blue suit hung around for another minute and then left. The stupid blond guy stayed put. I hated that guy.

Grandpa Victor covered his face with his hands and kept it covered. I wasn't sure what to do with my hands, they seemed so weird and robotic. Derek said he had to go pee. The blond man took my brother to a bathroom somewhere and they returned a few minutes later. Derek had grabbed a big stack of brown paper towels in the restroom. He gave us all some.

We kept waiting. Mom, who knew a ton more than she was saying, kept quiet. And I had a strange thought, that if all of us started pretending that Dad was okay then he would be okay, that the only reason he wasn't okay was because we were playing along with the idea that he was not okay, not challenging it, saying it was a big lie. Maybe if enough people say and believe that something true is false then it becomes false. Crazy, huh? I even thought that I should have never accepted the gingersnaps and soda from the airline people, because to accept food and other stuff from them was to also accept their lies, that my dad wasn't okay. I should have thrown the soda and cookies at the blond man and the red-haired woman and the man with the light blue suit. Refused to play along.

And then a man with slippery black hair and big teeth came into the room and shook our hands and patted us on the backs and said how sorry he was and he gave Mom a list of counselors available to help us "during your time of great need." All of the counselors were in the Columbus area, but we don't live very close to Columbus. The man then said that they were about to unload "your person," if we wanted to take a look.

Mom and Grandpa Victor glanced at each other and shrugged, then we all stood up and followed the man with slippery hair into a different room, one with a big window. There were some other airline people in that room, too, the man in the blue suit, two stewardesses, a guy who looked like a pilot or a copilot, and some other guy. I kept waiting for the pilot or copilot to give Derek and me silver pilots wings, like airplane pilots in movies give kids all of the time, and maybe pat us on our heads, but that never happened. We didn't get silver wings or pats on our heads.

Through the window we could see a big airplane, its nose aimed right at us. For the longest time nothing happened, but then a man wearing a gray suit and holding a walkie-talkie came out of the door, followed by two paramedics carrying a gurney with some guy on it, covered by a pure white sheet. We were supposed to believe that the man under the sheet was my dad, but I wasn't buying it. Could have been any dead guy under there. Or even a *CSI* actor playing a dead guy.

Everyone made it safely down the mobile stairwell — this wasn't an episode of *America's Funniest Home Videos* — then the paramedics set the gurney inside of a parked red and white ambulance, then one of them shut the door and checked to make sure it was latched. The paramedics climbed inside the ambulance, both of them in front, and drove away, no lights or sirens. The man in the gray suit waved to the paramedics then said something into the walkie-talkie, which we heard in the room, on a radio the man in the light blue suit was holding. The man on the runway said, "We're done here."

"Thanks, Alex," radioed the man wearing the light blue suit. In case you are just itching to know, Alexander is a Greek name that means "defender of men."

If a stewardess with long legs hadn't started talking I might never have gotten the true story about what happened to my dad. She said to Grandpa Victor, I think, or to all of us, "He was slumped over for the longest time, but we all just thought he was sleeping, like some of the other passengers were doing. He even had a little smile on his face like everything was fine. We didn't know."

"I'm sure you did your best," Vic said, patting the stewardess on the back. She started sobbing, like she had just lost a close friend, and then she bear-hugged Grandpa and then Mom and then Derek and then me. The stewardess smelled like ivy, and for a few dumb seconds I thought it was Christmastime. I wanted her to stop squeezing me and to keep squeezing me, at the same time.

"Be strong for your mother," said the weepy stewardess.

"I will," I said, not so sure that I wanted to be strong for anyone, that day or ever.

And then the man who was a pilot or copilot and who did not like to give out silver wings to kids asked how old Dad was.

"Just thirty-seven," said Vic.

"Thirty-six," corrected Mom.

"That's far too young for something like this," said the pilot or copilot. Almost everyone nodded, including me.

"Natural causes" were two words I would hear a lot of over the next few weeks. But there is nothing natural about losing your thirty-six-year-old dad. Most dads live twice that long, or longer. I believed then, and sometimes believe now, that some guy must have murdered my dad. Jabbed him with a poison-tipped umbrella while he sat in his airplane seat or slipped cyanide into his soda. Not because my father had done anything bad to him, but because he was one of the good people in the world. For evil people to rule they need to wipe out enough of the good ones, like Albert Garrett. Someday, I have told myself, I will become a great detective and investigate the murder and hunt down the killer. My invisibility should be a huge help. I could follow around suspects and gather clues without being seen.

Unless it was just natural causes. Then there would be no bad guy to catch and beat up and throw in jail. That wouldn't be right. Someone needs to be beaten up for what happened to my dad. Someone needs to rot in jail for a hundred years.

Anyway, at the airport I kept waiting for my dad, alive and well, to come out that airplane door and walk down those fourteen steps. But while I was waiting for this, the door was closed and then two airport workers in orange jumpsuits wheeled away the stairs.

Derek must have felt like I did, because after Mom signed some papers and we were on our way, my little brother threw a nasty tantrum, kicking and smacking Mom and Grandpa Victor and even me, and yelling, "We have to stay! We have to stay!" Mom and Vic tried to comfort my brother, or distract him, and so did I, reminding Derek that Henry the cat was waiting at home for us and she was probably very hungry, so we'd have to feed her two little cans of gourmet cat food, not just one. But no one told my brother to shut up. He was screaming what we wanted to be screaming. "We have to stay! We have to stay!" But we couldn't stay, waiting for a miracle that wasn't going to happen. We had to go home.

So now you know what happened to my dad. Wish it were a better story. Sorry. Wish it were a lie. Sorry.

55. The log of the Starship Finn Garrett, entry X

EARTH DAY OCTOBER 15, 8:28 P.M. Ugh. I hated that last chapter, every word and every drawing. But I am the keeper of my father's story. I need to share everything I know.

Turning off the computer . . . now. I'm going to find Derek, play some video games with him. Play until my fingers freeze up.

Go have some fun.

56. Escape to Firefly Island

Ready to go on?

On The Terrible Day That Changed Everything me and my family — what was left of it — made our way through the airport and to the car and headed home. Derek had calmed down some, but he still looked out the back window, toward the airport, even when it was no longer seeable. Grandpa Victor had to drive the SMV because Mom was a waste case. My grandfather cried a little while driving and said that thing about Dad being with us in the car, as a ghost. Derek, when we were still a long way from home, threw up in the backseat. Mom, most of the time, babbled "It can't be true" or shook her head or looked frozen, a robot without any juice. And I closed my eyes and sent myself back in time.

I went back to a night three summers ago, the kind of night where every cricket in the world seemed to be making a racket. My mom and dad and brother and I had gone for a drive in the country to see the farmlands and old red barns and lazy cows and horses and even a few emus. A world close to us but so very different from our own.

On the way home Derek and I fell asleep, like we always did. But I awoke to find that Dad had stopped the car somewhere and turned off the lights, and that he and Mom were gazing at a cornfield lit up by a zillion flickering lightning bugs. It was like watching the best show ever, for free. The flashing lights seemed like some kind of mysterious code, a song the fireflies sang to each other. It wasn't meant for us humans, but we were listening anyway.

"Wake up, kids, you might want to see this," Dad said.

"Already awake," I said. We decided to not wake up Derek. He can be a grump when he first wakes up.

Mom and Dad held hands, snuggled into each other. "This is a perfect night," said Mom. "One of the best ever."

"They are all perfect nights," Dad said. I wasn't so sure that was true, but I did know that I was living a perfect moment, one that I would not soon forget. Have you ever had a weird feeling like you unexpectedly walked into one of the highlights of your life, one that you'll probably want to tell your grandkids about someday or write about in your autobiography? It felt just like that, that I was living through one of my big, memorable moments, the kind that don't show up every day, no matter how hard we wish for them.

As we were enjoying the firefly flashes and the warm evening and each other's company, Derek's belly grumbled. We all laughed. The fireflies kept flickering, kept singing. And then, as if wanting to be part of the blockbuster show, daggers of heat lightning crackled through the dark July sky. That was a nice touch, completely unexpected. Mom *ooh*ed. Dad *aah*ed. And I had so much joy in me, I wanted to do cartwheels inside the car, even though I suck at doing cartwheels.

I stayed sheltered in that memory of a perfect summer night until Grandpa Victor pulled the SMV into our driveway and cut the engine and the lights. We all sat half dead in the car like crash-test dummies, unsure what to do with ourselves, unsure how to go on without Dad. Then Derek, brave Derek, crawled out of the SMV and began shuffling to the house. The rest of us did the same.

Heading to the house, dadless now, I swear I could feel myself starting to vanish. Just a few microns at first, going stealth.

Later that night, some of our neighbors brought food over to the house: cakes and doughnuts and a pizza and a roasted chicken and three or four kinds of pies. But we didn't need food, we had plenty of food. Cabinets and a refrigerator and a freezer in the garage packed with the stuff. We needed Dad.

57. Firefly factoids

1) Fireflies are actually beetles. Their species name is *Photinus pyralis*.
2) Some Asian fireflies have gills and can live underwater.
3) Baby fireflies eat earthworms, snails, and slugs, while the adults are believed to be vegetarians, feeding on plant nectar.
4) Baby fireflies use their lights to warn away predators. Adults use their lights to attract members of the opposite sex. Not all adult fireflies can produce light.
5) Some female fireflies will mimic the signal patterns of different kinds of lightning bugs in order to attract the males, and when the guys show up they will try to eat them! Male fireflies don't cheat like this. This tells you everything we need to know about girls.

58. A good guy doing a good thing

My dad was on that airplane because three days earlier he had flown to Boston to check on a childhood friend of his who had been beaten up and robbed outside a dance club in downtown Boston. Dad stayed with his friend until he was sure he was going to be okay, then he took a taxi to the airport and headed home.

I sometimes think this: If Dad's friend hadn't gotten beaten up, or if my dad wasn't such a good guy, had stayed home instead of going to Boston to see if he could help out his buddy, maybe the thing that happened never would have happened. Or if it happened here, in Sunnyvale, we would have gotten Dad to the hospital in time, saved him. And maybe we'd all be living in a different world, a world that includes my dad.

I'll never know.

59. When Wrights do wrong

I'm not too mad at the airline company anymore, though they really should keep a closer eye on their passengers and try to save them if they run into trouble. But I am still steamed with Orville and Wilbur Wright for inventing the first successful airplane. Should have stayed focused on their bicycle business instead of gazing at the sky and dreaming of being up there, among the birds and the clouds. Keep your eyes on the ground, guys. If God had meant us to fly . . . In case you are curious, Orville means "golden city," and Wilbur means two things: "will" and "fortress."

If there were no airplanes, then Dad would have taken a train or bus home and might still be around. You see, he passed away ten thousand feet above Earth, made it really easy for the angels or whoever claims souls to take him. If he had been on Earth, if the angels had to go to all of that trouble of descending to the planet, maybe they wouldn't have bothered. Yeah, this is another one of those "what if" things. There are a million of them. A million possible ways to save my dad.

60. Flight lessons

Don't be afraid of flight, okay? People almost never die on airplanes, of natural or unnatural causes. In fact, experts say it's the safest way to travel. Safer than trains, buses, and cars, and probably even safer than travel by skates and skateboards. Don't be afraid don't be afraid don't be afraid don't be afraid. Promise me? Flight is magical. Just ask any bird . . .

any butterfly . . .

any bee . . .

But don't ask penguins or ostriches or chickens. They have mixed feelings about flight.

I've only flown twice in airplanes, both times when I was a little kid. I hardly remember those trips, the first one to Washington, D.C., for a family vacation, and the second one to Jacksonville, Florida, to visit Grandma Beatrice and her friend Harold. His name means "leader of the army," but I don't know if that particular Harold ever led any armies. And I'll fly again, as soon as I get the chance. I won't be scared, stepping foot on the airplane. Or if I am scared I'll do it anyway. Something Mom once said to me: Fear is a ferocious monster or it's a pesky little bug. We decide. (Huge clue: Make it a bug.)

And then maybe in twenty years or thirty years I'll

board one of the first spaceships bound for the colonies on the moon or on Mars. Won't that be a total buzz. *The New Adventures of Space Boy.* Look out for the asteroid, Space Boy!

61. I like your wings

Airplanes are needed because people don't have wings. But what if people did have wings? What if, one day, pterodactyl-sized wings grew out of everyone's shoulder blades?

Do this: Imagine that you suddenly have wings.

Keep imagining.

Don't stop.

Keep going.

One more minute.

Today's extremely important question: Where did you fly to?

62. All twisted inside

When my family and I were at the airport on The Terrible Day That Changed Everything, as we all waited in the back room, the man in the light blue suit said, "How are you doing, champ?" The question was thrown in the direction of Derek and me, but I was the one who caught it. Even though I didn't hate the man in the light blue suit as much as the blond guy with doll's hair, I still wanted to punch him in the nose and kick out half of his teeth, and then say, *I feel like that, but on the far inside.* Instead, I said, "No comment."

If you have lost people you loved, even a favorite pet, then you know that feeling, like someone is twisting your guts and squeezing your soul, and no matter what you do or say they won't stop squeezing and twisting. A day, a week, a month later, they're still squeezing and twisting you, but maybe not quite as hard.

I'm still being twisted and squeezed, four months later. I'm tired of it. Stop it. Leave me alone.

63. Last gifts

Two weeks after The Terrible Day That Changed Everything the airline finally delivered Dad's luggage, a black leather suitcase and a blue carry-on bag. In the suitcase were some gifts my father had bought for us in Boston: for Derek, an official Red Sox cap signed by a third baseman I never heard of before; for Mom, an opal necklace, the opal shaped like a heart; for me, a big bag of saltwater taffy. You see, my dad knew that I have a sweet tooth as big as one of those model teeth you find in the dentist's office, the one the hygienist uses to show you how to brush away the gunk.

Mom keeps her opal necklace locked away in a jewelry box, and Derek keeps the baseball cap on his dresser, not on his big square head. But me, I eat at least one piece of taffy each day, chewing it slowly and stretching it out and making it last as long as possible. I think Dad would have wanted us to enjoy the gifts, not hide them away or let them gather dust.

The soon-to-be-here crisis: I'll be out of taffy in twelve days, or before then. When that day comes, should I eat the last piece or try to keep it forever? What would you do?

64. The log of the Starship Finn Garrett, entry XI

EARTH DAY OCTOBER 17, 10:26 P.M. Just reread the last several chapters. Man, are they sad. Wonder if anyone will want to read them, or if they'll even like my book. *Skip the middle of the book,* they'll tell their friends. *It's a total bummer.* I wish this were one of those stories where even though there are some struggles and problems, nobody dies. Someday I will write that better kind of story.

So now what? Where should we go?

65. Time capsule

Let's go here. "Love is the glue that holds us together." Dad said that once, when I was little. Isn't that deep? Isn't that true?

Try this: Make a list of everyone and everything you love. Show it to someone you love, then hide the list for ten years — lock it in a safe or bury it in a jar or a can in your backyard — and then look at the list again, as your older self. Do you still love those people and things? Are there people and things you want to add to the list? Good luck with this assignment, soldier! No peeking for ten years.

66. Zombie days, zombie nights

I can't tell you much about the four days following The Terrible Day That Changed Everything, except that I now have a pretty good idea what it's like to be a zombie, or maybe a *Blade Runner* replicant without much humanity programmed into its motherboard. I wore clothes and I looked a little weirder than usual and I stumbled around. That was about it. My mind and my soul, most of me, had shut down, had flown away, were gone. I ate and I slept and I wore clothes and I looked weird and I stumbled around.

Our house was often filled with way too many people — I do remember that. Neighbors and close relatives and some distant relatives and people from Mom's bank and Dad's sporting goods store, and even a few of Dad's high school and middle school teachers and coaches, some of these intruders saying and others thinking that Mom and Derek and I shouldn't be left alone "at a time like this," not letting us decide that for ourselves. They threw a lot of hugs and handshakes and cheek kisses our way. Not many of them stuck.

During the reception, the thing they have after the burial, my uncle Trevor, Aunt Meredith's new husband, let out a killer, room-clearing fart. That kind of thing would normally cause Derek and me to laugh while running for cover, but I'm pretty sure we didn't do any laughing while running for cover. The name Trevor means "big village." He really should be named Shamim, not Trevor. Shamim is an Arabic name that means "odor."

The funeral service and the "viewings" were held at Chapman Funeral Home in downtown Sunnyvale, kitty-corner from the public library. The building looked pretty cool from across the street, but if you got close to it you could see that the tall pillars in front were made of plastic, not stone, and that whoever painted the black shutters did a lousy job — you could see the brushstrokes. Also, there were a few weeds and grass blades in the flower gardens, pushing through the brown mulch. Dumb! And inside the building most of the carpet, including in the main viewing room, was dark orange, which I thought was kind of weird. It hurt my eyes, to look at that carpet for more than a second. Plus, the heavy fake flower smell of the pot-pourri in the boys' bathroom gave me a headache. There should never be potpourri in a boys' bathroom! For all of these reasons I cannot recommend the Chapman Funeral Home of Sunnyvale, Ohio.

There was a three in the afternoon viewing and a seven at night viewing. Viewings are when people walk by the dead guy in the casket and look sad and think sad thoughts. Hardly anyone showed up for the three o'clock service, but the seven o'clock one was packed, standing room only. Derek wore a gray suit and I was in a black suit that was too thick for the warm weather, and Mom wore a black dress she had to borrow from a coworker at the bank because she didn't own any black dresses, and Dad, or his clone, the dead guy in the casket, wore a dark blue suit. Derek's suit was one or two sizes too big — it used to be my suit when I was his age — so it was easy for him to hide his hands, which he did most of the time, and the pant legs had to be rolled up an inch.

The casket was open during the funeral and the viewings, which I thought was really stupid. Seeing someone dead messes with your memory of them as a living person. It almost pushes you out of your body — it's that terrible.

Dad was smiling as he lay there in the casket, but I think that was something the funeral home people did, smooshed his face that way. No way would he be happy about leaving us and the world so soon. At least his coffin looked cozy, for a long rest—lined with thick white satin.

During the viewings Derek and I were supposed to stay seated with Mom and Grandpa Victor and Aunt Meredith and Uncle Trevor and Uncle Jacob and our two girl cousins, Kaylee and Brianna (their names mean "slender" and "noble")—they are Meredith's kids from her first marriage—but most of the time we roamed around the funeral home, checking out rooms that weren't being used, or we hung around outside. There was a little patch of bright green grass in back, between the parking lot and a row of shrubs, which we claimed as our own. Hunted for bugs. Waited for it all to be over.

An ashtray and a pen I stole from the funeral home

The next morning there was a service at Chapman Funeral Home where a man in a brown suit who did not know my dad very well stood behind a podium and said some nice things about my father. Don't ask me what, I hardly remember being there. Then everyone jumped into cars and SUVs and pickup trucks and headed to Green Oaks for the burial. About sixty or seventy people were at the cemetery, including some folks who never made it to the viewings or the service at Chapman Funeral Home. Grandpa Victor called only showing up for the burial "cutting to the chase." I called it cheating. Reverend Hollingsworth from the Presbyterian church we hardly ever went to said some nice words about my dad and even nicer words about God. It was all too real and unreal at the same time, and I wanted to be anywhere else in the universe but there. Derek and I had to sit near the casket between Mom and Vic — I think we all held hands — but when the services were over and people were talking and hugging and crying, Derek said he really wanted to climb a tree, that he had to do that right away, so we checked out several trees in the area, mostly pines and a few oaks and maples, but none of them had low enough branches, even if I gave my brother a big boost. I think the cemetery people cut off the low branches so dopey kids like us wouldn't climb their trees and fall off and break an arm or two and sue them. And then it was time to go.

On the way home, just a few blocks from our house, Mom, who was driving the SMV, weirdly said, "We should keep driving until we run out of planet." Sounded good to me, but we didn't do that. Mom drove us home and we had the reception, which lasted the rest of the day. It all went pretty smoothly, I think, until around eight o'clock when Derek came into the living room, where most of the intruders were gathered, and said, "Where's Dad?"

Just about everyone lost it, a total sobbing festival, including Mom and Grandpa Vic, but not me. My brother's no pea-brain, he knew where Dad was: Green Oaks and heaven. A couple hours later Derek told me he had meant to ask, *Where's Henry?* — he had wanted to play with the cat — but the word "Dad" slipped out instead. It's pretty funny, if you think about it.

And that's about all I can remember from those zombie days. I didn't feel even slightly like myself until the fifth day, when Melanie stopped over and we played catch and then I spied on her, finally getting away from the house for a few minutes. Maybe someday more memories from those freaky and mostly missing four days will flood back. I sure hope not.

67. A chapter that does not exist (where'd it go?)

I need a serious break. Do you?

Go on, set this book down and run around like a spazzed-out nutcase. Or build a birdhouse out of Popsicle sticks. Or write your own book. Or turn your closet into a space capsule or your space capsule into a closet.

Come back when you're ready. See you later.

Hey, why are you still reading? We are on official time-out here. See?

68. A true story about a vanishing boy, part VI

By the sixth or seventh day following The Terrible Day That Changed Everything, I had about a dozen white hairs on my head, and my skin was decently chalky. A zombie I still was, but with a beating heart and a half-working brain.

One day in July, while looking at my reflection in the bathroom mirror and counting white hairs, I realized that I was being slowly erased for my big sin — failing to save my dad. I'm not sure how I was supposed to have saved my father, just that I was supposed to. Maybe made sure he ate more vegetables and exercised more so "natural causes" didn't stand a chance. Or kept him from going to Boston, somehow. Whatever it was, I failed to do it and Dad paid a huge price and I was paying a smaller price. Disappearing from the world, hair by hair and skin cell by skin cell.

But now I just don't know. Kids aren't normally in charge of saving their dads. The reverse, dads saving their kids, happens all of the time. Looks like another theory has bitten the dust.

69. The log of the Starship Finn Garrett, entry XII

EARTH DAY OCTOBER 20, 10:02 P.M. In the space capsule with Commander Derek Garrett and Corporal Henry deKat, zooming through deep, dark space at warp 99. Our mission: to travel faster than light, faster than time, and return to Earth at least one year younger, to a world that includes our dad. This is a risky mission, never before attempted. If we go too far back in time, to before we were born, we may cease to exist.

"Fasten your moon belt," I say to Commander Derek. "This is a rough patch of space we're passing through."

"Look out for the giant purple thingamajig, Captain!" he says.

"Thanks, Commander," I say, steering us clear of danger, for now. "That was a close call."

Meanwhile, Corporal deKat is manning the solarscope while also washing her face with one of her mutant, catlike paws.

Update: The mission has failed. My copilot, Commander Derek, has fallen asleep, and Corporal deKat is nudging at the escape hatch with her furry little head, wanting out.

Maybe next time.

10:38 P.M. Can't sleep. Wander downstairs. Find Mom in the den, going through a big box of photographs of our family and her family and Dad's family.

"Did I ever tell you how I met your father?" Mom says, looking sad and happy at the same time.

"Sure," I say, "you met at one of his college baseball games."

"No, that's your dad's version of the story," she says, "where he comes off as Casanova in a baseball uniform. The truth is we first met at an old-fashioned sock hop."

"What's a sock hop?" I ask. In my head I'm seeing all kinds of socks hopping around. Maybe the goal is to grab as many of them as you can. The kid with the most socks wins.

"It's where you dress up like they did in the 1950s," Mom says, "and dance to music from that time. Chubby Checker, Buddy Holly . . ."

"What was so great about the 1950s?" I ask.

Mom shrugs. "Probably nothing, but sometimes it's good to pretend."

And then she tells me the story.

"I had gone to the dance with a couple of friends of mine, but it was really dead. There were maybe twenty people at the gym, nearly all of them girls. Hardly anyone was dancing.

"Anyway, I spotted your father standing in a corner by himself. He was wearing a leather jacket, a white T-shirt, and blue jeans, and his hair was slicked back. He'd want me to tell you that he looked just like James Dean, but to tell the truth, he looked more like Squiggy from *Laverne & Shirley*. Have you seen that show?"

"Maybe on Nick at Nite," I say. "Or TV Land."

"So I went over to that handsomer version of Squiggy and asked him to dance," Mom says. "He was reluctant, said he owned three left feet, but I talked him into it. On the dance floor we slow-danced to a slow song, and then to a fast one. As it turned out, your father was right, he wasn't much of a dancer, but he could handle the box step.

"At some point your dad told me he played shortstop on the college baseball team. He said that their next game was that Saturday, so I asked him to hit a home run for me. He laughed. 'I'm not much of a power hitter,' he said, 'but I'll give it a try.' Oh. For the record, he did not kiss me that night, at the sock hop. I would have liked it, but he just sort of left the gym while I was freshening up. Not exactly a Casanova!

"So I went to the game. The first time up, your dad struck out on three pitches, and the second time he hit a pop-up to the infield. I was worried that my being there was making him nervous, and maybe that was true, because he also flubbed a couple balls in the field, though he did also help turn a killer double play, which had most of us fans jumping up and down and cheering.

"When he was due for his final time at bat, while he was waiting on deck, I got as close as I could to your father and reminded him of his promise. 'You better hit that home run or there will be hell to pay,' I said. Something like that. All your goofy father did was smile and point to the left-field fence. It was really cute.

"At the plate your father swung wildly at the first pitch, which wasn't even close to being a strike, and he did the same thing for the second pitch, but this time he really connected. The ball went sailing high into the sky, toward the left-field fence, and I was thinking, *He did it, he hit a home run for me*, but then the outfielder from the other team caught up to the ball and snagged it maybe five feet from the fence, and that was that. No home run, game over."

"And that's when he asked you out," I say.

"No, no, that's your dad's version of the story," Mom says. "I asked him out, right after the game, to my dorm room for a dinner of microwave tacos. Let's just say that sometimes your father needed a little nudging. Make that a lot of nudging. But that was when we started dating, that night of the game and the night of our first kiss."

Mom is suddenly looking more sad than happy.

"Good story," I say, wondering which version of how my parents met, Mom's or Dad's, is the true one. In Dad's story a teammate dared him to ask out the prettiest girl in the stands, which happened to be my mom. I think I like that one better.

"Wait, there's more," Mom says, cheering up a little. "There were only two more games that season, and your dad didn't hit any home runs. And then that summer, when things got serious between us, he quit the team, which, just so you know, was completely his idea. But anyway, before and after we were married, when your father was in one of his moods or was otherwise taking himself too seriously, I'd sometimes say something like, 'You still owe me that home run, you know,' and three times out of four that would pull him out of his funk."

Smiles.

"So why did you come downstairs?" Mom asks. "Need a snack?"

"I came for that story," I say, which, for once in my life, seems like the perfect thing to say.

Bigger smiles. And then Mom gets back to digging through the pile of old photos, and I run upstairs to write these words down before my body forces me to sleep.

70. The letter

I forgot to tell you that sometime in early August we got a letter from the man Dad went to visit in Boston. His name is Lowell Grimes. He grew up in Sunnyvale, that's how he knew my dad, but then he moved to Boston after graduating from high school. Dummy. Lowell means "wolf cub," and grime means "dirty, filthy, repulsive scum."

The letter was addressed to Mom, but she showed it to Derek and me. Lowell wrote a whole bunch of things we already knew about Dad, like he was great and kind and wonderful and generous, and he said that he felt "somehow responsible" for what happened, since Dad had flown there to see him, to make sure he was okay. Good. Lowell Grimes should feel responsible, since what happened was all his fault. He ought to have never gone to that dance club where he was beaten up and robbed. He's a grown man. Going to dance clubs is for college kids. He should have stayed home and watched TV, like other grown men who aren't married do.

And Lowell wrote that he had asked Dad to stick around a few more days, until he was strong enough that they could hit a Red Sox game together, but my dad said, "Sorry, I'm a family man. The wife and rug rats have to come first." That was the only cool part in an otherwise dumb letter.

That's all he wrote. If you ever meet a man named Lowell Grimes from Boston, Massachusetts, please give him evil looks and call him a giant farthead. He deserves it.

71. Mad money

Besides the letter, Lowell Grimes also sent us a check for $300 "to help pay for obligations," whatever that meant. Mom cashed the check the next day and gave Derek and me $25 each. "Mad money," she said. "Go have a little fun." But I didn't want to have fun with that dirty money, so I gave my share to Melanie. She bought a pair of studded jeans at the Sears store at the mall in Ashton City.

I'm not sure what my brother spent his $25 on. Think I'll go ask.

Answer: candy, Goldfish crackers, and baseball cards.

72. The big, big game

I was planning to spend the afternoon at the cemetery but they were having a burial, and the dead person must have been someone really well known because there were hundreds of sad people in nice black clothes at Green Oaks and the line of cars stretched the length of the graveyard. No room for me.

So instead I went to Melanie's basketball game. It was the Sunnyvale Middle School Mighty Hornets versus the Madison Junior High School Mustangs. Both teams had six wins and two losses and both teams hate each other. It was the big, big game. I even pretended that I had a whole bunch of school spirit. *Go Hornets, sting the Mustangs! Give them an allergic reaction!* (I didn't actually yell that but I did loudly think it.)

I wore a hoodie to the game so no one would stare at my old-man hair and at my dead-guy skin, but people stared anyway. And a boy who was seven or eight came and sat next to me in the stands and asked if I was a rock star, and if I was could he have my autograph? I told him no, sorry, I'm not a rock star. "But I am turning invisible," I said. "I should be completely vanished by Christmas. The first kid to ever disappear." His eyes grew large and he asked again for that autograph. I gave it to him, signing a grammar test he had gotten back from his teacher. I signed, *To the coolest kid ever, from Finn Garrett, The Last Invisible Boy.* The kid thanked me then carefully folded up the paper and left.

After he jumped off the stands he looked back and waved. I waved to him then yelled, "Hey kid, what's your name?"

"It's Rex," he yelled, looking a little embarrassed. I suppose that these days more dogs than kids are named Rex.

"Your name means 'king,'" I said to him. "You're the king of Sunnyvale." That seemed to make him happy.

And then a few minutes later I heard two gossipy ladies talking about me.

Lady 1: "What do you suppose is wrong with that boy over there? Anemia? Some kind of vitamin deficiency?"

Lady 2: "The white one?"

Lady 1: "No, the green one. Of course the white one."

Lady 2: "Do you always have to be snippy like that? Maybe nothing is wrong with him. Maybe he just dyed his hair that color."

Lady 1: "And his skin, too?"

Lady 2: "Sure, why not. It's probably the latest thing, the almost-out-of-blood look. Anemic chic, or something like that. You know how kids are these days. Tattoos, piercings, blue hair . . ."

Lady 1: "Or he could just be an albino."

Lady 2: "Are you an idiot, or do you just play one on

TV? Albinos have pink eyes and white eyelashes. That boy's eyes and eyelashes look perfectly normal."

Lady 1: "Could be a partial albino."

Lady 2: "There's no such thing as a partial albino!"

The ladies stayed silent for a few sweet seconds, were probably busy making ugly faces at each other. But then:

Lady 1: "He could have been touched by an angel. That's what turned him white."

Lady 2: "Or by the devil."

Lady 1: "Oh wait, I know what it is. I bet he suffered some kind of terrible shock to his system."

Lady 2: "That's probably just an urban myth, that an emotional shock can make your hair go white."

Lady 1: "You're an urban myth!"

They kept yakking. I wanted to reach down their throats and rip out their voice boxes, or at least hit the off switches, but instead I covered my ears and sang a children's song in my head, "Puff the Magic Dragon." I used to love that song when I was a little black-haired, pink-skinned thing, crawling and walking around this corner of the planet. Mom would sing it, Dad would sing it, or we'd all sing it together. That song always made me feel so calm.

73. Finn's coming-out party

After trying to hide myself for nearly an hour, and failing, I finally gave up during the third quarter of Meli's basketball game, pulling down the hood of my hoodie. *Ta-da!* More people in the stands and some of the ones roaming around or watching the game from the floor stared or at least gazed at me now and then, and a few of them even rudely pointed. One older boy sitting in the stands backed away when he saw bleached-out me and fell out of the stands and landed on his butt. I thought that was kind of funny. The worse starer was a girl who must have been from Madison because I was pretty sure I had never seen her before. After five minutes of her looking at me like I had just dropped in from Jupiter to check out an earthling basketball game, I turned and snapped at her and growled like a rabid dog. *Grrrrrrrrrr.* The girl jumped out of her skin and then jumped back in. But she stopped staring.

Early in the fourth quarter my friend Benjamin showed up and sat down next to me. That took a little courage.

"Hey," he said.

"Hey," I said.

"Hey again," he said.

"Shut up," I said.

And then we played the old smash-our-legs-into-each-other-until-someone-says-"ouch" game. It's probably not the best game.

"Not to be mean, but you totally look like a ghost or a vampire, something kind of dead," Ben said during a break in the game—a skinny girl from the Mustangs was hobbling off the court.

And I said, "Boo!" to Ben, and I thought, *Ghosts eat toast and live mostly on the coast.* And then I wondered again if my dad was a ghost I cannot see. A watcher of the world, like the owl at the cemetery.

After a game of elbowing each other in the side until someone said "cut it out," Ben left for a leaf-raking gig. Twenty bucks, which doesn't sound too bad, but when you do the math that's like one hundredth of one cent per leaf.

Near the end of the big, big game, the Hornets down 54-53, Melanie stole the ball from one of the Mustang girls and raced toward her basket, dribbling around a defender and outrunning two Mustang players who really, really wanted to catch her, and did an easy layup.

Easy for her—I would have blown the shot. It was really amazing, what she did, something you'd see in the pros. Even though there were still eighteen seconds left on the clock, the Mustangs couldn't score any more points before time ran out and the Hornets won the big, big game 55-54.

Later, as Meli and I rode our bikes home, she said, "I could see you the whole time when I was dribbling to the basket, you know, because you're so white and stuff, you really stand out. It made me run faster. Technically, you should get an assist. You helped us win the game."

I thought about that for a few seconds. "I was a lighthouse and you were the girl sailor lost at sea. I guided you safely to shore. I mean the basket."

"Yeah, something like that," she said.

I thought some more. "I was the silvery moon and you were the lost traveler," I said. "My light helped you find your way. To the hoop!"

"Not bad," she said. "But I like the first one better."

And then we raced home. I won, by a pale nose.

When I went inside my house and into the kitchen I nearly had a freak attack. Mom's hair was totally white, just like mine. Was she turning invisible too? Could my entire family be vanishing? Six weeks from now people in Sunnyvale will be saying, *Whatever happened to the Garrett family? It's like they just disappeared.* There will be movies and TV specials about us and a hundred different ghost stories.

"I bleached my hair so we'd be a matching set," Mom explained, smiling and poofing her hair up with her hands. "What do you think?"

"You look beautiful," I said. I felt something icy inside of me melt away, and then some of that ice water made it to my eyes. Mom hugged me like we hadn't seen each other for ten years.

That's when Derek, home from his judo lesson, came into the kitchen and blankly gazed at us. "I'm living in a horror movie," he said. But overall, my little brother didn't seem too upset about that.

Mom offered to bleach Derek's hair white but he said he wanted to keep his hair his current color (muddy brown). Party pooper. Mom and I then debated whether to bleach Henry the cat's fur, then agreed that Henry would rather not be bothered. As you might have figured out by now, we are all pretty weird over here.

74. Finn's Amazing Water Tales, part III

After dinner I had to carry six garbage bags and the recyclables' bin to the curb so the trashmen would pick them up in the morning. At my house I get all of the glamour jobs.

When I was finished with the chore, and as I was heading back to the house, it started to rain. Just a few chubby drops at first, but then it poured like crazy, like Mother Nature had cranked open the rainwater valve as far as it goes. I stood in the middle of my yard during the storm, got soaked to my bones. "The Last Great Undersea Boy lives!" I shouted. I felt clean, standing in the rain, like God was hosing me off, washing away a ton of muck.

The storm moved on, to the east, to hose off some kids in Tuttle Township and Newbury Falls. I went inside to change my soppy clothes, and when I looked in the bathroom mirror, I saw that a little pinkness had returned to my skin. I told it to leave. The pinkness waited around for a minute or two and then followed my orders and left. I just wasn't ready.

75. Quiz time

Ready for a pop quiz? Several explanations have been offered for my freaky hair and pale skin and my nearing invisibility. Did you catch them all? Please choose your favorite explanation from the list below:

a) I'm turning into a living ghost so I can hang out with my dad.

b) All my crayons have been stolen, except for the black and white ones.

c) I'm an experimental kid.

d) Spending too much time at the cemetery is whitening my body.

e) I'm experiencing a "healing crisis."

f) I'm turning myself into an old man so that I will soon be with my dad.

g) I have the worst case of adolescence ever.

h) I want to be invisible so I can solve Dad's murder.

i) I'm going supernova, just like a star.

j) I want to be like the hero Perseus and slay Gorgons while I'm invisible.

k) I am becoming a replicant, a vampire, or a living zombie.

l) I'm being erased for failing to save my dad.

m) I'm suffering from a disease or a vitamin deficiency.

n) I've had a severe shock to my system, and/or my soul was smacked.

o) I'm a partial albino.

p) I've been touched by an angel, or maybe by the devil.

q) All of the above.

r) None of the above.

Which is the correct answer? Who knows if we will ever know. Some very important things can stay a mystery forever. Like how life started, and if it exists on other planets. Like how some people, like Meli, can brighten up a room just by showing up. And possibly like what the heck is happening to Finn Garrett.

Another reason this whole thing could remain a mystery: The lead detective on the case, that's me, is only twelve.

76. Before there was Finn there was Timmie

I finally had a chance to see the 1957 movie *The Invisible Boy*. I guess it's not a very popular film, I couldn't find the video at any of the video stores, but the city library was able to borrow it from a library in New Philadelphia, Ohio. The movie had some cool moments, but overall it pretty much sucked.

The Invisible Boy is a make-believe story about a freckled ten-year-old boy named Timmie, who becomes friends with Robby the Robot. There is also an evil supercomputer that has the power to control both of them. Timmie and Robby build a giant radio-controlled kite together, which is kind of cool, and Robby keeps Timmie's dad from spanking him, which is more than you can normally expect from a robot. Robby also has the ability to turn Timmie invisible, and when he does this Timmie uses his powers to spy on his parents (in their bedroom!) and to take revenge on a neighborhood bully. The second half of the movie is mostly about the evil computer, but near the end of the story Timmie and Robby the Robot board a nuclear-armed rocket heading to the moon. Timmie's dad doesn't want to let his kid fly to the moon, but he has no choice because if he goes against the computer's wishes the computer will use the rocket to destroy Earth. The end.

Besides being a pretty dumb story, I thought *The Invisible Boy* didn't really show what it feels like for a kid to disappear from the world—instantly, like Timmie, or slowly, like me. Sure, there are the good parts, like spying and being able to get away with pranks, but what about the bad parts, like being unseeable by people you love? Or what if once you are totally invisible there is no way to make yourself visible again? That would stink. Unless you are totally bored and have nothing better to do, I wouldn't bother watching this movie. Should anyone ever make a film about my freaky life, *The Real Invisible Boy* or something like that, hopefully it will be a lot more entertaining. End of review!

77. Who's the daddy?

One night a few weeks after the funeral, when Mom had crashed and Derek and I were playing video games, my little brother said, "You're kind of the daddy now."

"The heck I am," I said to Derek, and then we got back to playing Backyard Baseball and then Shadow of the Colossus. But maybe the smelly little rat had a point. With Dad gone, I am now the oldest male in our family. I guess I better start working out, lifting weights and doing push-ups, in case I ever have to beat up a burglar or something daddyish like that.

Truth? I'd rather just be a kid.

78. The log of the Starship Finn Garrett, entry XIII

EARTH DAY OCTOBER 22, 11:02 P.M. Just ate a piece of saltwater taffy, lemon swirl, and thought about my dad buying me the bag of taffy in a market somewhere in Boston. Only three pieces of dad taffy remain. Help!

Sleepy, but I think I'll stay up for a little while and work on this book. Here's a drawing:

The view from my bedroom window

79. Grandpa Vic comes for a visit

We hadn't seen Grandpa Victor for a couple weeks so Mom invited him over for dinner. Normally we don't eat a lot of red meat around here, or much meat at all, but my grandfather insists he's a "meat and potatoes guy," so Mom made meat loaf and gravy, with mashed potatoes, buttery green beans with almond slivers, and dinner rolls. It was one of those heavy kinds of meals that sinks you deep into your chair and makes you feel like you're made out of granite.

After dinner Grandpa Victor was in a storytelling mood. That can be good or it can be bad. Sometimes when he's finished with his stories it seems like I'm coated in dusty old memories that aren't my own. I have to shake them off.

Today my grandfather told us stories about Dad when he was little, like how he had a favorite teddy bear named Truman that he'd lug around with him wherever he went. "You'd pretty much need the Jaws of Life to separate those two," Grandpa said. "I suppose they were best friends, if such a thing is possible. They never wanted to be apart."

"That's how it was when Albert and I were dating," said Mom, her eyes wet and twinkling, like gemstones under water. "We couldn't stand being apart from each other."

You were each other's Truman the teddy bear, I thought but didn't say. Truman means "trusting man."

Grandpa Victor smiled at Mom and nodded, but he didn't seem in the mood to share the storytelling stage with her, so he quickly jumped into the next tale, saying that up until my dad was twelve or thirteen, he always seemed to be falling off wagons and scooters and bicycles, his knees and elbows ever skinned or scabbed. A klutz. My dad was a klutz. "If he was only wearing one Band-Aid that meant he was having a good day," Vic said. "Five or six bandages was more typical. I swear that kid could trip over air."

I've seen dozens of photographs and even some faded, jumpy movies of my father when he was a kid, smiling for the camera or waving or looking irritated that a camera lens was aimed at him, but while Grandpa was talking about some of Dad's more serious spills I tried to imagine my father actually living his life when no one was photographing or filming him. It was a big imagining that required my entire brain. What did my dad look like when he didn't think anyone was watching? I wondered. I could see Dad when he was about eight, riding his banana-seat bicycle down a gravel and tar road, gravel pinging against the fenders and chain guard, but then for no apparent reason he crashed into a tree and went flying off of his bike. And I could see him when he was about five, riding in a red wagon that some curly-haired girl in a polka-dotted dress was pulling, but then for no known reason the dumb girl suddenly made a sharp turn and Dad went tumbling out and skinned a knee. Darn it! Am I doomed to always see my father having these little accidents, now that I know he was a klutz? Thanks, Grandpa.

Vic then told us some stories about my father's teen years, saying that he had "unexpectedly turned into a bit of a rascal." During the summer when he was sixteen, Dad spray-painted peace signs and smiley faces on people's mailboxes, and got in trouble for pulling up surveyors' stakes in a woods that was going to be dug up so a ritzy housing development could be built. "Albert said he was trying to save the trees," Grandpa said, shaking his head. "I didn't get it. They were only trees."

I got it. Trees can't run or fly away or hide themselves when the bulldozers show up. They need people like my dad to save them. People like me. People like you?

Go hug a tree. I'll wait. No trees close by? Try hugging a utility pole, a basketball pole, a nonprickly shrub, a store mannequin, or even a living human being you are fond of. If all else fails you may follow the instructions below for the tricky self-hugging procedure.

Step 1:

Ready your arms

Step 2:

Fold them around yourself

Step 3:

Smile and feel the love

80. A new friend that just happens to be a tree

After Grandpa Vic was finished yakking I had one of my greatest, most outstanding ideas of all time: Since Dad was so into trees, we should buy a tree and plant it in his memory. Everyone liked the idea, so we all hopped into the SMV and drove to a garden center in Newbury Falls to find just the right tree. On the way there Vic told us some more Dad memories—there was no shutting him up. We were now up to my father's college years, right before he met Mom.

"Sure, Albert had some big career dreams, hoped to coach professional baseball or even play it, if he could raise his batting average ten or twenty points," Vic said. "But once he met your mother you could say that his priorities quickly changed. The main thing he wanted to do, the only thing he wanted to do, was marry Enid and start a family. Fortunately for you guys your mother agreed to it. I tell you, as a husband and as a father, I've never seen a man so completely happy."

We all cried, listening to the story, including tough little Derek, even though we had heard this story before. It was the good kind of cry, the kind that shivers your insides with happiness, but it was also a little bit weird. When you cry inside a moving car you can't exactly jump out and run to your room and hide yourself. All of us are used to crying alone.

The garden center had hundreds of trees to choose from — little trees and medium trees and big trees, some with dangling fruit or berries or pinecones or flower buds — and it wasn't easy deciding which one to buy. Derek wanted to get a blue spruce, a little Christmas tree, but they were really expensive and no one was sure how Dad felt about pine trees, if they were his favorite kind of tree. Mom wanted to get a pink or white dogwood, but the garden center man said it wasn't the best time of year to plant flowering trees, with winter nearing. Grandpa Victor suggested a pear tree because it would provide shade and something tasty to eat, but Mom said all of that fallen and rotting fruit in the yard would cause a big, smelly mess. And I wanted to get a weeping willow — yeah, I know, mega symbolic — but they only had two willows left, and both of them were kind of spindly and looked unhappy, even for weeping willows. So after all of that debate we decided on a baby elm tree, a tree we all liked but weren't exactly gaga over.

We bought the tree and took it home — sadly, it rode by itself in back — then as the sun was leaving for the day Grandpa Victor planted it in the backyard, in Dad's memory. After setting the bundled elm in the hole he had dug, Vic tied three straps to the base of the tree and anchored the straps to metal stakes he had pounded into the earth. So the tree grows tall and straight, Grandpa said to my brother and me, and to help it survive windstorms and other threats. I wasn't sure, but I guessed that the "other threats" might be my brother and me, running around in the backyard.

Derek and I packed fresh topsoil and peat moss around

the tree, and Grandpa Victor sprinkled some tree food, and Mom dragged out the garden hose and watered the elm. Then we all gathered around the tree and held hands while Mom said a little prayer.

"This is for you, Albert," said Mom, her voice a little choppy. "Wonderful father, loving husband, and sweet man. You will never be forgotten. May this tree grow strong and tall and live many, many years."

And Derek said, "Miss you, Dad."

And I said, "Thanks for the taffy, and for everything else."

And Vic said, "Be at peace, son," then he sighed for so long I was worried that he had sprung a serious leak.

Each of us said "amen" and sniffled some, then we dropped hands and Mom and Grandpa Victor and Derek went into the house, planning to play a "rousing game of Yahtzee"—my grandfather's words. I stayed outside, hanging out with the first stars and visiting with the memory tree. I told it more about my dad, and the story behind my weird hair and skin—"I'm really not a little old man, honest," I said—and that soon I will be totally invisible, unless I can find a cure. The elm tree didn't have a whole lot to say.

So yeah, I talk to trees. Get over it.

81. To Vic or not to Vic, that is the question

Grandpa Victor left for home while I was still visiting with the elm tree, then a few minutes later Mom came outside to check up on me. "Thought you might have fallen asleep," she said, an ounce of worry narrowing her eyes.

"Just catching some moon," I said. That's something Dad used to say — "We are catching some moon" — when he and Derek and I would camp out under the stars on warm summer nights. No tents, just sleeping bags on the lawn so you had to worry about creepy-crawlies and sudden storms moving in. Usually it was just us guys plus Henry the cat. Mom isn't a big fan of creepy-crawlies and sudden storms.

And then my mom surprised me by asking how I'd feel about Vic coming to live with us. "Victor is spending far too much time by himself in that big house of his," she said, "and we could use a little more help around here. So what do you think, good idea or bad idea? Maybe if it works out we'll all be happier."

"We're doing okay," I said.

"We are?" Mom said.

"I think so," I said. "Pretty okay."

Mom thought about that for a few seconds and then had more to say. "If Victor does stay with us and pays some rent . . . well, let's just say that our money is getting tight lately with just the one income. Not that you should be worrying about these kinds of things."

"If I can sell my book we'll have that money," I said. "And I'm sure I can find some after-school and weekend jobs." Rake leaves this month, shovel snow next month.

"Book? What book?" Mom said.

So I told her about this book, how it was mostly about Dad but also about our lives since June and before June. Why had I kept the book a secret? I didn't want Mom to know about it until I was pretty sure I could finish it. Nothing worse than disappointing your parents, except maybe disappointing yourself.

"That's why you've been filling up journals and sketch pads," Mom said, smiling. "Far freaking out."

"Right on," I said, trying to fit in.

And then Mom said we could wait a few more weeks before deciding whether to invite Grandpa Vic to come live with us, that we'd talk it over some more and ask Derek his opinion. I nodded like a nodding goof.

The truth? I'm kind of hoping Vic keeps living in his own house. I love the old guy, but he's so stuck in the past it's easy to forget there's a present world and a future world when he's around. But I kept my mouth shut, just in case Mom and Derek would be happier with Grandpa living here. One time out of every thousand I do the right thing.

82. Sunken ship of memories

After Derek went to bed, Mom said she had something to show me that might help with my book, so I followed her to the dusty, cold, and spider-happy basement storage area. It's the creepiest area of the house. There might even be some rats and bats living in there.

"It's your dad's treasure chest," said Mom, pointing to an old wooden chest that looked like it belonged in a sunken ship at the bottom of the ocean.

Mom fiddled with the latch and opened it, and there was plenty of treasure inside. Not gold and diamonds, but Dad's baseball uniform from college, some of his favorite books, an old typewriter, report cards and school essays from middle school and high school, merit badges and patches from when he was a Boy Scout, a Little League baseball with its cover half torn off, a bunch of love letters and cards Mom and a few other girls had sent him, and locks of someone's charcoal black hair.

"That's some of your hair from when you were six or seven," Mom said as I held the little Ziploc bag full of hair up to the light. "From right after your father gave you a haircut."

I instantly remembered those Saturday-morning haircuts that Dad used to give Derek and me. He was a pretty good barber, never accidentally cut off our ears or poked out our eyeballs, and the price was right: free. And I remembered that I used to be a normal black-haired kid. And I remembered that I used to be totally visible. And I remembered that I loved those days.

I spent another five minutes going through Dad's treasure chest, but that was about all I could take for one night. There was too much of my dad in that old box, too much of the things he loved. I'll go back when I'm ready for more.

"At least we still have our memories," Mom said, after I closed the chest and latched the latches. "And no one can take them away from us." True, we still have the memories of my father. Hundreds of them. Maybe thousands.

And I decided, as I was climbing the steps with my mom, that my third book will be called *Finn's Book of Sweet Memories*. The book will be about all of our lives, not just about my Dad, everything I can remember that's worth writing about. I better start writing the memories down tonight, before some of them get ants in their pants and fly away. Before they are lost like tears in rain, as Roy the *Blade Runner* replicant would say.

83. Memory No. 326: Digging to Voleville

Note from Finn: Here, just for you, is an exclusive preview of my third book.

I only remember my father yelling at me once during our time together on Earth. I think the fact that he hardly ever became upset with me was due more to his personality than to me being the perfect son. I messed up a lot. Broke things, brought home stray animals, left doors open and lights on, sometimes got bad grades. But only once did Dad yell.

It was a warm summer day, late July or early August, and I was nine and a half years old and on my way to ten. Bored out of my mind, I was digging up part of the backyard, hoping to find a live animal that lived underground, a mole or a vole or a gopher or a groundhog, or maybe tunnels or an underground kingdom where several of the beasts lived. Or find buried treasure—that would have been okay too. Or colorful old bottles and pottery from a century ago.

When Dad came home from work and saw me tearing up the yard, he yelled, "What the hell are you doing to my beautiful grass?" I froze in place. When someone who hardly ever raises his voice is suddenly screaming it can really shake you.

"Well?" Dad said, not letting me stay frozen. "Answer me!" It was true that my father spent a lot of time caring for the lawn, mostly by spreading fertilizer and chemicals every couple weeks, though later, after Mom talked him into it, he went organic. And here I was ruining it. I felt about three inches tall.

"Finn, I asked you a question," Dad said loudly. "What are you doing to my grass?"

"Nothing, I'm doing nothing," I said, starting to tremble with fear, but I was also a little bit mad. I thought it was my grass too, not just Dad's. All of ours. And I was only digging up and exploring a small part of it. My part.

As my father watched with judgmental eyes, I filled in the small holes I had dug and then stomped the turf back down. Finally, Dad went inside the house and I no longer felt so stressed and microscopic, but I was still bummed out. I must have done something really stupid for my quiet dad to wig out. I normally didn't think of myself as a stupid kid, but would a stupid kid be smart enough to know that he was stupid?

When I was done repairing the damage as best I could — that part of the yard still looked more like a patchwork quilt than a lawn — I quietly slipped inside the house and went up to my room. I cried and felt dumb and small and misunderstood and completely on my own. I was even making plans to run away that night, after everyone else had gone to sleep. I thought I might try living in New Mexico. It sounded like a sunny and friendly state.

I had been in my bedroom for about a half hour when my dad knocked on the door and then came inside, holding two shovels. "So what are we digging for — oil?" he asked, smiling a smile that could only be called goofy. "Black gold? Texas tea?"

"Moles or voles," I said. "Or a groundhog or a gopher. I want to see where they live."

"We'll probably have to dig pretty deep," Dad said. "We better get started."

So we went back outside and dug up the part of the yard that I had been tinkering around in, and a couple other spots. During one of the digs my father apologized for yelling at me earlier. "I had a bad day at work," he said. "But I should have left that at work." Dad sometimes came home flustered from the sporting goods store, especially on days when he had to deal with angry customers or had to fire one of the salespeople for messing around too much or for stealing money from the register. I knew it wasn't his dream job but he was pretty good at it.

"It's okay," I said to my father. "I should have asked first before I started digging."

He shook his head. "You're a kid. Kids dig up stuff. Just be a kid."

Later Derek came outside and helped with the digging, but he was still kind of little so he used a trowel instead of a shovel. Now and then one of us would take a rest, supervising the other diggers or searching through the dug-up soil, looking for treasure or fossils. Sometimes Mom watched us from the other side of the kitchen window, and once she brought out iced sweet tea for us to drink. We dug until it got too dark to see what we were doing, and then we stopped and went inside.

We didn't find any animals or underground tunnels, or fossils or hidden gold, but we did find an old buffalo nickel from 1936 and maybe an arrowhead, or it could have just been a pointy piece of flint. I still own that hunk of flint—Derek kept the nickel—and sometimes when I hold it tight, it seems like that summer night that Dad and Derek and I dug up the backyard comes back to me in nearly its entirety, like the memory is held in the flint, not in me.

And just the other day I decided that it was in fact an arrowhead, not just a triangular piece of flint. Probably used by members of an Indian tribe who spent most of their lives underground, living in a network of tunnels they had dug and in caverns. The famous Vole Hunters tribe of central Ohio.

84. The log of the Starship Finn Garrett, entry XIV

EARTH DAY OCTOBER 24, 10:31 P.M. Another day ends. Before going to bed I ate the last piece of saltwater taffy that Dad had bought for me in Boston, enjoying the chewy blast of cherry-flavored sweetness he had wanted me to enjoy. The candy is gone, but I will keep forever the last wrapper, that wrinkled and sticky piece of yellow wax paper.

EARTH DAY OCTOBER 25, 12:09 A.M. Can't sleep. It's a warm night for this time of year. Decide to put on more clothes and go for a walk. Escaping from the house is pretty easy these days. Mom is usually zonked out on sleeping pills, and Derek, if he sees me, won't tell.

Outside. I start walking. The moon follows me. So do a handful of stars.

In front of Melanie's house. Normally her bedroom light is out this time of night, but tonight it's shining. I wait for her to look out the window. Wait some more. And some more. And some more. Consider tossing a stone or a penny at her window. Worried I'll break the glass.

Finally Meli comes to the window and looks out. Shakes her head and smiles and waves at me, all at the same time. I do two of those things, smiling and waving. She sticks her tongue out at me and makes a funny face. I do the same. She waves again and then disappears. Her room goes dark. I wonder what she'll dream about tonight.

Start heading home. Think of the fact that Meli could see me, standing in her yard like a lovesick monkey. I want her to be able to keep seeing me, without the need for infrared goggles. I want to stay visible.

Block from my house. A car, an old Pontiac, slows, and some dumb high school kid, one of five kids packed in the car, yells, "It's the ghost of Marilyn Monroe!" Another kid wolf-whistles at me. They speed off. I am not the ghost of Marilyn Monroe.

Home. Derek is sitting on the porch, in his baseball pajamas. I go up to him.

"What's it like?" he says.

"What's what like?" I say.

"Walking around in the middle of the night," he says.

"Let's find out," I say.

My little brother stands up, then we slog through the dewy yard and begin walking around the block, on the side-walk, sometimes concrete, sometimes sandstone. Breaking curfew laws, but oh well. Derek gazes at the moon and stars. He gazes at some dark trees. He takes my hand.

"It's not too scary," he says.

"Hardly scary at all," I say.

We keep trudging along.

"Dad would have liked this a bunch," Derek says. "Walking in the night."

"Yep," I say, feeling my insides warm a little.

About halfway around the block, halfway home, Derek slumps, slows down.

"You okay?" I say.

"I'm pretty sure I want to be sleeping again," he says.

So I pick my brother up and carry him the rest of the

way. Not quite as heavy as he looks, or maybe I'm stronger than I think I am. Derek quickly falls asleep. The moon follows us. So do some stars.

Home. I take my brother inside and put him to bed.

85. She's got skills

Just as I was dozing off I was awoken by clacking sounds and a bell noise coming from downstairs. I slid out of bed, stumbled down the stairwell, and decided to investigate.

Mom was in the dining room, typing on Dad's old type-writer, the kind without any plugs or memory chips. A tall stack of blank paper and a steaming cup of coffee were close by. I figured that my mother had either forgotten to take her sleeping pill or she was weirdly sleep-typing.

"What we used to type on in the Stone Age," Mom said, glancing at me and looking a little wired. "I hope they still make ribbons for this model."

"Writing a book about Dad?" I asked.

"About your father, about love, life, family, everything that's important," she said. "You're not the only one with writing talent in this family, Finn. I used to be quite the wordsmith when I was your age, and a little older."

"Cool," I said, unsure if this was a project my mother was going to stick with, or if a couple days from now the book and the typewriter would be collecting dust. But it was sweet to see a spark in Mom again, even if part of it was caused by coffee.

My mom turned a knob that caused the page she was typing to be spat out, and then she turned it the opposite way and rolled in a fresh piece of paper. "Oh, sorry," she said, "is the noise keeping you awake?"

"I'm fine," I said. "Good night."

"Night," she said, starting to type again.

I retreated to the kitchen and watched Mom type from there for a minute or two. It looked like she was in a race to tell some kind of giant truth about life that would save the world. I silently wished her luck.

Back in my room I was worried that the typewriter sounds would keep me awake, but instead they were kind of soothing, for some dumb reason. I quickly fell asleep.

86. A true story about a vanishing boy, part VII

Early this morning I had the freakiest dream. It started in black and white and many shades of gray. I was driving with my dad somewhere, in an old, weird car, maybe a Model T, but I was the one driving and Dad was the passenger. First, we were on a highway with hundreds of other cars and too many lanes to choose from, some of them rising into the clouds, and then we were driving though the Green Oaks Cemetery, but not on the road because there was no road, and then I was dropping Dad off at his store. "Have a good day, Mr. Finnski," Dad said as he was crawling out of the car. "Catch you later," I said to my dad, or something just as stupid. "No need for that,"

Dad said. "Besides, I'm too slippery to be caught." He winked at me and walked away. I watched my father disappear inside of his store. It looked like they were having some kind of blockbuster sale. There were balloons, a clown or two, and hundreds of customers. Even though I was sad about leaving Dad behind, I put my foot on the funky accelerator — it was shaped like a bear's paw — and drove off.

Then, when I was driving on my own, but in a Jeep or a convertible, some kind of car without a roof, there were suddenly rainbows all over the place. Not just in the sky, but everywhere. Ribbons of colored light were prettying the black and white and gray world, bringing it to life. Bands and strings and ropes and taffy threads of every color were wrapping around trees, chasing after cars, tying themselves around houses and apartment buildings and schools, colorizing and brightening everything, including me: My arms, what I could see of them, looked very fleshy. It was like part of my brain had broken out the crayons and watercolors that had been hidden away since early summer. I woke up mumbling some kind of gibberish, and sobbing.

I got out of bed and stumbled into the bathroom and looked at my reflection in the medicine cabinet mirror and saw that five, no six, make that seven strands of my hair were black again, not white. "Hello, living hair," I said in a soft voice, not wanting to scare away the black hairs. And I noticed that my skin had a little bit of pinkness to it, some life. I did not tell it to leave. I did not want it to leave. "Hello, sort of better skin," I said. My hair and skin had nothing to say.

Like a weirdo in love with himself I kept staring at my reflection. Could color-happy Crayon Boy be slowly replacing Invisible Boy? I wondered. I have no clue. But time, that blabbermouth, will tell.

And then, after brushing my teeth, I ran back into my room and drew a dumb comic strip for this book.

Meet Crayon Boy

I told you it was dumb. It's not like you weren't warned.

87. A nearly normal breakfast

I didn't think Mom or Derek would notice the changes —
I was still mostly a white-haired little freak — but at the
breakfast table Derek gazed at me oddly and said, "Who
are you and what did you do with my brother?"

Before I could come up with a funny answer, something
involving alien abduction or cloning gone bad, Mom nodded at me and said, "Welcome back, kiddo." Even Henry
the cat, hoping for dropped crumbs or charitable handouts,
seemed to be looking at me funny, showing that "I know
everything there is to know in the world" kind of smile
that cats like to smile.

"It's good to be back," I said, waving my hand like a king
greeting the commoners and having to bite down on my
tongue to keep from crying away the last of my tear water,
to keep from becoming dried-out Desert Boy.

And then we ate breakfast, my mother and brother and me. We had mushy cornflakes in soy milk, banana-nut muffins (slightly burned but still tasty), and pineapple juice that made my lips pucker. Dad was still missing, from the breakfast table and the house and from everywhere else you would normally find him, but I knew he was somewhere, flying above mountains or growing green branches or maybe racing motorcycles in heaven. Gone, but not even close to being forgotten.

88. The log of the Starship Finn Garrett, entry XV

EARTH DAY OCTOBER 25, 7:50 A.M. Sunny and warm. "Indian summer," they call it. I seem to be coming alive. Too early to know for sure.

I get ready for school then quickly check the bathroom mirror again and discover at least twelve living black hairs, and counting. Yes! I dash out of the bathroom and downstairs and find Derek waiting for me in the living room, clutching his backpack. "Let's go, shrimp," I say. He stands up, and we walk out of the house and across the lawn, heading toward his bus stop at the end of the block.

"Do you remember going for a little hike last night?" I ask my brother as we march down the sidewalk.

"That was my dream," he says. "How did you know?"

"It was my dream too," I say.

"That's pretty bizarre," he says.

I hang out at the bus stop until a few responsible-looking parents show up to wait with Derek and the other kids, then I jog back to my house and grab my backpack, kiss Mom good-bye, then dash outside to the memory tree and touch one of its branches and wish it a happy day. And then I run to my bus stop, one street over on Oakwood.

Melanie is waiting there, glowing bright light on pale me. She smiles as she studies my hair and my face and my arms. Seems to be thinking big thoughts.

"You look less ghosty," she says. "Good work."

"Thanks," I say, feeling a little less ghosty.

A minute later the bus pulls up and the door folds open, and Meli and I climb aboard. And here I am now, sitting on the creaky school bus next to Meli and writing the last words of this chapter in my notebook. AND WRITING THIS. And writing THAT.

The usual stares from the usual kids. Big deal.

Melanie shifts in the seat so our legs touch. Little fizzes of light sparkle in the air around us, like they sometimes do when Meli and I are this close. "You really should draw a picture of me," she says, grinning and showing her teeth.

"Sure thing," I say, reaching for my backpack and hunting through it for my sketch pad and an art pencil.

I think it just might be a pretty good day.

If you are ready for this book to end, turn the page. If not, please set this book aside until you are ready, or go back to the first page or someplace in the middle and start reading again.

I'll wait while you make up your mind.

89. To be found in the "all good things must come to an end" department

My name is Findlay Abner Garrett. My father was light.